ALSO BY PHILIP R. CRAIG

VINEYARD BLUES

A Martha's Vineyard Mystery

PHILIP R. CRAIG

SCRIBNER
New York   London   Toronto   Sydney   Singapore

SCRIBNER
1230 Avenue of the Americas
New York, NY 10020

SCRIBNER and design are trademarks of Macmillan Library Reference USA, Inc., used under license by Simon & Schuster, the publisher of this work.

Text set in Baskerville

Manufactured in the United States of America

ISBN 0-684-83455-3

For my son,
Jamie,
who shares Martha's Vineyard
with his parents.
A skeptical mind and a sentimental heart
is not a bad combination.

Devouring Famine, Plague, and War,
Each able to undo mankind,
Death's servile emissaries are;
Nor to these alone confined,
He hath at will
More quaint and subtle ways to kill;
A smile or kiss, as he will use the art,
Shall have the cunning skill to break a heart.

—JAMES SHIRLEY
from *Cupid and Death*

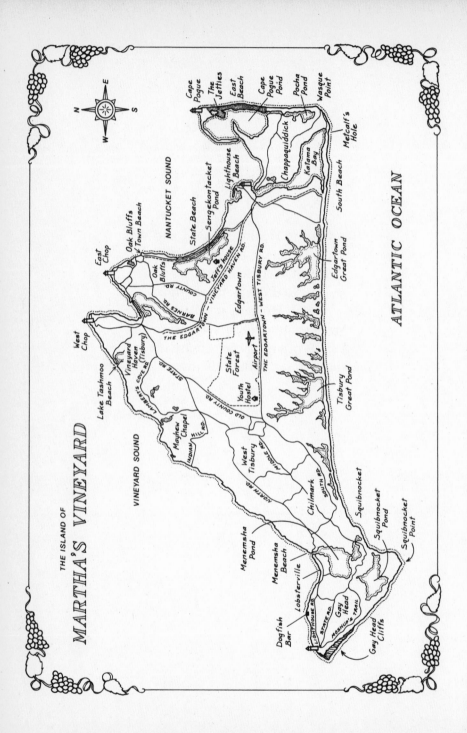

— 1 —

The first time I saw Corrie Appleyard I was about five years old. I woke up hearing music late at night and came downstairs and found him and my father sitting in the kitchen of our house in Somerville, picking at their guitars while Corrie sang. The next time was about a year later in a dingy bar somewhere in Boston. My father, my sister, and I were at a table and Corrie was on the little stage, sitting on a high stool behind a mike, playing and singing. I remember that it was a smoky, smelly, noisy place and that I was drinking an orange soda, and that we were the only kids there, but I don't recall much else. Later, Corrie used to come to our house whenever he was in the Boston area, and a couple of times he came to my father's cottage on the Vineyard. Then I didn't see him anymore until June this past summer, when he came walking out of the past down our long, sandy driveway.

Zee and I and the kids were in the yard loafing under the warm blue June sky when Diana stopped running around and stared up the driveway, then moved over to her mom. Zee and I turned our heads and there was Corrie walking toward us, satchel in one hand, guitar case in the other. I hadn't seen him in more than thirty years, but I recognized him instantly. At first, he didn't seem to have changed at all, but then he'd always looked ancient to me, being older, even, than my father.

Now, though, he really did have some years stacked on his shoulders. His skin was still that same coffee color, but now it was lined and his hair was mostly gray, as was the mustache and beard that once had been black as tar. There was a hint of illness in his face, but though his step wasn't quite as light as it once had been, it wasn't an old man's shuffle, either. It was the stride of a man who had walked a lot and still had places to go.

He hesitated as I stood up from my lawn chair, but then came on.

"Who could that be?" asked Zee, giving cautious Diana a hand to hold.

"That's Corrie Appleyard," I said, feeling happy. I went to meet him and put out my hand. "Corrie," I said. "My God, it's good to see you."

He put down the satchel and squinted at me as he took my hand. "You got the edge on me, young fella. Who might you be?"

"I'm J. W. Jackson. Roosevelt's son. You used to come to our house in Somerville and you came here once or twice, too."

His smile was as white as ocean foam. "Little Jeff. You've growed up some. Well, I'll tell you, Jeff, I happen to be on the island, so I thought I'd come and see your daddy." He looked at the house. "My, my, this place has changed quite a bit."

I picked up the satchel. "It was mostly just a hunting camp when you were here, but now it's getting closer to being a house. You won't find my dad, I'm afraid. He died a number of years ago. But come on, I want you to meet my wife, Zee."

He walked beside me. "Rosy, dead? I'm sorry to hear it."

"It was a warehouse fire. A wall fell on him and a couple of other firemen. Almost twenty years ago, now. My sister's married and living out near Santa Fe, and I'm right here. We sold the Somerville place."

He shook his head. "Twenty years. Time does fly."

We came to where Zee and Diana were standing. Zee, wearing shorts and a shirt tied around her flat, tanned belly, held Diana's head pressed against her with one hand, while Diana wrapped both arms around her mother's sleek thigh and eyeballed Corrie, trying to decide whether he was friend or foe.

"Zee," I said. "This is Corrie Appleyard. Corrie, this is my wife, Zee."

Their hands met and their smiles gleamed. "How do you do, Mrs. Jackson?"

"Call me Zee, Mr. Appleyard."

His head dipped and rose. "Zee, then. And I'm Corrie. I knew your husband's father, and Jeff, here, when he wasn't much older than that lad over yonder. I do believe that you're the first Zee I've known."

"It's short for Zeolinda. My people are Portuguese."

"And Corrie's short for Cortland. My people are mostly African originally, with little bits of this and that mixed in over the years. And who might this be?"

"This is my daughter, Diana. And that guy over there is her big brother, Joshua. Joshua, come and meet Corrie."

Joshua, who had been taking things in from the far side of the yard, came and accepted Corrie's hand.

"How do you do?" said Corrie.

"I'm fine. Nice to meet you," said Joshua, just the way he'd been taught.

"You shake hands, too," said Zee to Diana, "and say hello."

Diana let go of her mother's leg with one hand and held it out. "Hello," she said.

"Hello, Diana." Corrie's big brown fingers enveloped her small pudgy ones.

Diana retrieved her hand and again wrapped her arm around Zee's leg. Her eyes went to Corrie's battered, sticker-covered guitar case. "I know what's in there."

"What?" asked Corrie.

"A guitar."

"You're right," said Corrie, acting impressed. "How did you know?"

"My pa's got one. He plays it sometimes."

"Does he, now." Corrie looked at me.

I nodded. "I have two, actually. My dad's old Martin, and a Gibson I got at a yard sale for thirty bucks. But to call what I do with them 'playing' is stretching it a bit."

"He sings to us sometimes when we go to bed," said Joshua, who as usual had been listening even though he didn't have a lot to say.

Atta boy, Josh. Stand up for your old man.

"I was about to bring out some lemonade for the kids and a couple of beers for the grown-ups," said Zee. "You got here just in time to join us. You and Jeff have some catching up to do, I'd say."

"Well, I don't mean to intrude on you, but a beer sounds good. Thank you."

"Don't say too much before I get back," said Zee, lifting Diana to her hip. "I want to listen in." Mother and daughter turned and disappeared through the door of the screened porch.

"Let's grab a couple of chairs," I said, and led Corrie to the lawn table between the house and the garden. He put his guitar case on the ground and sat down.

"I remember the view," he said, looking east over the garden toward Sengekontacket Pond, the barrier beach on its far side, and the sound that stretched toward Cape Cod.

"A million-dollar view and a two-thousand-dollar house," I said. "Like the guy in the song with a ten-dollar horse and a forty-dollar saddle."

He nodded. "I remember when Rosy bought this place. Twenty-five hundred dollars, as I recall. He wanted me to go in with him. Did you know that?"

"No. He did, eh?"

"Yeah, he did. Your mom was dead then, poor thing, and Rosy wasn't interested in any other woman. He thought the two of us could share this camp, but I had the Mississippi place already, and a sugar foot to boot, so I wasn't interested in owning anything I couldn't carry with me. Besides, I told him, there wasn't no reason for me to spend all of my money buying a house when I could sponge off of him for free! So he bought it by himself." Corrie's laugh came from deep down somewhere.

"Well, you're more than welcome to stay here now, if you don't mind tight quarters," I said. "A lot of water under the bridge since I last saw you, and we'll need some time to catch up."

But he was looking at the lumber in the yard and at the skeleton of the rooms I was building for Diana and Josh, and shook his head. "Not this time, but thanks. I see that you've outgrown the place and are adding on. I'll have that beer and then be on my way."

I felt a wave of dismay. "You can have the couch in the living room. I don't want to lose you before you're really here."

"That goes for me, too," said Zee, coming out with a tray filled with drinks, crackers, and bluefish pâté. "We've about worn out that record we have of you and Blind Boy Fuller, and I want to spend some time with the man who made that music."

"That's mighty fine of you, ma'am, but I already got me a place to stay. Boy I know and some of his friends living here in a big house for the summer, and I got a bed there waiting for me. But I'll be pleased to sit a spell and catch up on the news. Say, isn't that bluefish pâté? I remember your daddy used to make that and it's got my mouth watering."

"Well, don't wait around for an invitation!" said Zee. "Pitch in before we eat it all ourselves."

Zee sat herself down and we all got into our beer and food.

"Mighty fine," said Corrie, smiling. "So you still got that old bootleg record, eh? Must be pretty worn by now. I gave it to Rosy almost forty years ago."

"It is wearing a little thin," I said, "but we just don't listen to the scratches." I nodded at his guitar case. "I'm glad to see you're still at it."

"And I'm glad to see you got yourself a nice family and are settled down. I remember I got a letter from Rosy just after you lied about your age and went off to Vietnam. You wasn't the settling-down type back then, and your daddy was worried about your wild ways."

"And not without cause," said Zee, circling my arm with hers. "But I've got him under my thumb now, and I'm trying to civilize him."

"I see that you are, and I want to hear all about everything before I leave you." He dug a small plastic vial from a pocket and shook out a pill. "My doctor probably wouldn't approve of me washing this down with beer, but I do a lot of things he don't approve of." He laughed and popped the pill into his mouth.

So we talked and had more beer and finger food, and talked some more as the summer sun fell away to the west.

I told him about my very brief combat experience and the wounds I'd taken in Nam, about recovering and coming home and joining the Boston PD and going to school and getting married and divorced and shot and recovering again but giving up the save-the-world game and moving down to the Vineyard and meeting Zee.

And Zee told him about growing up over in Fall River and becoming a nurse and marrying and supporting her husband Paul (known to me as Dr. Jerk) while he studied medicine until, studies behind him, he'd left her for a more adoring woman and she had come to the island and met me and married me and now we had two little Jacksons to support us in our old age.

And Corrie told us how he wandered from down south to up north and from out west to back east, always playing in small clubs and bars, never making it onto the big stages and never minding that at all because the real blues people knew who he was and what he could do, and that was enough since the music had always been the important thing. He had no ego, for when he talked about his music, it was as though his talent were one thing and he himself was something else; the talent was a gift that had been entrusted to his care, and to which he owed a duty. He was only its caretaker, and took no credit for possessing it. As he tried to explain this, I was reminded of hearing Pavarotti talking about his voice ("the voice," he called it) in the same way, as though it were something apart from himself, toward which he had the duties of a caretaker.

Corrie talked of appearing with Josh White in Boston back in the fifties, and meeting my father there in the club and coming home with him because he was short of money and Rosy had offered him a place to stay. He told of hanging around in New York and playing with Brownie McGhee and Alec Seward, and learning from the Reverend Gary Davis, and listening to Larry Johnson, who was young then and still was by Corrie's standards.

And now he was on the island so he could play at the coffeehouse up in Vineyard Haven and later at a church in Oak Bluffs.

"I read about that in the *Gazette*," said Zee. "We'll be there to listen. I wouldn't miss it for the world!"

"Mighty fine," said Corrie, looking at the house. "You folks have spruced this place up a bit. You still have fishing rods hanging on the ceiling like when Rosy and I used to come down here? That man sure knew how to catch and cook a fish. We had some good times out on the beach."

"The rods are still there," I said. "Maybe you'd like to go with us in the morning. I have to meet somebody here at ten, but the tide will be right about seven, and we plan to do some fishing before I need to be back. We'll be pleased to have you go with us."

He smiled and nodded. "And I'll be pleased to accept that offer." He glanced at the sky and the lengthening shadows. "Well, I gotta be on my way." He stood and put out his big brown hand. "I thank you for your hospitality, Zee."

"It's been my pleasure. You're sure you won't stay?"

"No, ma'am. I thank you for the invitation, but I've got people waiting for me. I'll see you in the morning. Been a long time since I went after a bluefish." He reached for his guitar case, but I had gotten to it first.

"I'll drive you," I said, walking toward my old Land Cruiser and snagging his satchel as I went.

"I know a kidnapping when I see one," said Corrie with a laugh. "Good evening, Zee."

"Good night," said Zee, watching as we got into the ORV and drove away.

"Beautiful girl," said Corrie.

"She is that. Where are we going?"

He got out a piece of paper and named a number and a street in Edgartown. "Grandson of a friend of mine is living there with a bunch of his college friends," he said. "Down here to try to make some money before he heads back to school this fall. Says they got an empty bunk I can have as long as I need it."

The Vineyard teems with such young people every summer. Most of them enjoy the sun, sand, sex, and other island entertainments before going back to the mainland in time for the fall term, and some of them actually manage to save some money in spite of the outrageous prices of the outlandish accommodations offered by the local slumlords.

The house where we stopped looked to be typical of such places. It was old and run-down, and its unkempt yard was littered with beer cans and other collegiate debris. There were five cars and a moped in the driveway, a fairly good sign that the occupancy limit was being totally ignored.

Corrie climbed out and collected his gear, then leaned down and stuck his hand through my window.

"Thanks for the ride, Jeff. You know, you look a lot like your daddy did thirty years ago. See you in the morning."

"Check out the escape routes before you hit the sack," I said. "One of these places burned down last March. They're all tinderboxes."

"I've seen worse. Thanks for the ride."

He walked toward the house and I drove home, feeling good. Corrie Appleyard. Who'd have thunk it? I'd not read a paper for a week, and thus had missed the ads for his concerts. If he hadn't decided to visit my father, I might never have known he was on the island. More evidence that the nonliterate life was not good for me.

2

We were right on time the next morning, and Corrie was waiting for us. He climbed into the backseat with Diana and Joshua and we headed for Daggett Street and got in the ferry line.

"Times have changed," observed Corrie as we inched ahead, waiting for the little On Time ferry to cart cars three at a time across the channel to Chappaquiddick. "Used to be we drove along South Beach to get to Chappy."

"A sore point," said Zee. "Don't get J.W. too wound up on that issue."

Too late. I was quick to be annoyed. "Dad-blasted environmentalists keep the beach closed all summer these days. No ORV's allowed, the theory being that the beach is being ruined and the plovers and terns are going to be killed by people driving by. Bunch of hogwash! The ocean wears the beach away, like always, natural predators kill the birds, like always, and now everybody has to go to Chappy by this ferry, so in the middle of the summer the waiting lines reach halfway back through town and we have to hire extra cops just to tend traffic!"

"He gets testy about this subject," explained Zee in her best wifely voice.

"Damned right!" I said.

"You can tell he feels very virtuous," said Zee. "He thinks most environmentalists are idiots."

"Not most," I said, "some. The sanctimonious ones, especially."

"The ones who get between him and what he likes to

do," said Zee, smiling back at Corrie. "He's not very good at having other people tell him how to behave."

True. The ferry took three more cars and the line moved ahead. I put my hand on Zee's thigh.

"I'm getting to be one of those guys who always talks about the old days," I said, looking at Corrie in the rearview mirror. "You know the type. Why, when I was a boy everything was better than it is now."

"I don't want to hurt your feelings," said Corrie, "but as far as I'm concerned, you can have the good old days. I remember them pretty well, and I don't think I want them coming back again. Besides, in another few years these will be the good old days."

"By then I'll probably remember this as a golden age," I said.

We laughed. What nuts people are. Me in particular.

The On Time pulled in and we drove aboard. To our right, Edgartown harbor opened to the west and south; to our left was the lighthouse, the outer harbor, and the channel leading out to Nantucket Sound. There were moored boats both east and west of Chappy, and the falling tide was running strong. A southwest wind rippled the water, and the blue summer sky arched overhead like the inside of a Chinese bowl. We pulled away from the dock and crabbed across to the other side.

Years before, according to accounts I'd read, a fire truck on its way to fight a blaze on Chappy had tried to disembark from the ferry with such urgency that it had succeeded in spinning the boat right out from under it and standing itself on its rear end right in the ferry slip. We, being of more cautious bent, got off without incident and headed for Wasque Point on the far southeast corner of the island.

Wasque, like all coastal points, comes and goes according to the whims of the sea gods and goddesses. It gets bigger one year and smaller the next. Over the decades it has grown or shrunk as much as a quarter of a mile. A century or so before I was born, according to old charts, it was much farther out to sea than it is now, but the bluffs inland from the present point show that at some time it was a lot smaller. Whatever its size and shape, it is one of the best bluefishing spots on the East Coast, thanks to the Wasque rip that snakes out from the point, tossing bait around and attracting the voracious blues.

We fetched the point in time to catch the west tide, pulled up out of the reach of the slapping waves, and got the rods off the roof rack. There were already a half-dozen trucks ahead of us, and there were fish lying under them. Paul Schultz, who roamed the beaches for the Trustees of Reservations and always knew where the fish were but didn't always have time to stop and catch them, was driving out as we drove in. He waved and we waved back.

"You guys stay up here," I said to Joshua and Diana. "Watch out for cars, and don't get behind anybody who's making a cast. You don't want to catch a hook on somebody's backswing. Josh, you keep an eye on your little sister. I'll be back in a couple of minutes." I walked down to the surf, where Zee and Corrie were already fishing, and made my cast. The redheaded Roberts arced long and high and hit the roiling water with a satisfying splash. I took a couple of turns on the reel, glanced back to make sure that my offspring were doing what I'd told them to do, at least for the moment, and turned back to the sea.

The Roberts bounced and wobbled toward shore, offering an apparently attractive sight to any bluefish that might be around. I have caught more blues with it than with any other lure. However, there were apparently no fish close by at the moment, so my first cast was to no avail.

Down the beach there were a couple of bent rods, proving that there was life in the sea in spite of my failure to catch any of it. I hauled in and made another cast, and as I did Zee's rod bent and she set her hook. She looked at me and grinned.

"Land him," I said, feeling happy.

"I will," she replied and did. By then the fish had moved a bit closer to us, and both Corrie and I were on and working our fish toward shore. We got back to the truck at about the same time with our fish—nice seven- and eight-pounders.

"Like old times," grinned Corrie, "but I must be getting old. This guy almost wore me out!"

"Your fishing muscles are out of shape," I said. "You spend all your time with your guitar and none with a rod."

"Pa," said Josh, touching my arm, "I want to fish."

"Like father, like son," said Corrie approvingly.

I got Josh's little rod off the roof rack. He wasn't able to cast far enough to catch anything today, but you're never too young to try.

"Don't forget to throw the bail," I said. "You don't want to snap your lure off."

"I remember," said Josh in his solemn little voice. He took the rod and went down to the surf near his mother. She gave him a smile. If he ever learned to fish as well as she could, he'd be able to hold his own in any company.

Diana, alone now, grabbed one of my fingers. "Play with me."

"If you'll excuse me," said Corrie, "I'll get back to fishing. Maybe I can get a couple more of these fellows and take them back to the boys and girls in the house. I don't think they're much in the way of cooks, but they got an oven and I can show them how to bake a fish."

So then there were three of us fishing and two of us up on the beach playing a game I didn't quite understand, and it was a fine day.

When we headed back for home along East Beach, we had as many fish as we needed and a few more. I planned to smoke some of mine and sell the extras at the market to help pay for gas. Who knows, we might even make expenses for the trip.

"You have to come for supper tonight, Corrie," said Zee. "The boys at the house can do their own cooking."

"More likely they'll get some of the girls to do it for them," said Corrie with a laugh.

"No doubt," said Zee with a sigh.

"Well, if we can eat early, I'll be glad to come," said Corrie, "but I got to be at the coffeehouse by nine, and if I come to your place, you got to come to the show afterward."

"That's a deal," said Zee. "Win-win for us."

"For me, too," said Corrie. "Things do work out at times."

We sold the extra fish and dropped Corrie off with the three he'd caught. I handed him a fillet knife, since I doubted that there would be one in the house.

"I'll use this on these fish and put them in the fridge, then I got to put in some practice," said Corrie, leaning over the driver's-side window and looking in at us. "Old fingers ain't as limber as they used to be. Got to keep 'em loose."

"I'll pick you up at five."

"What a dump," said Zee as we drove away. "There ought to be a law against renting out places like that. They should make Ben Krane live in one of these slums he owns!"

"There is a law," I said. "It's just that there aren't enough cops to enforce it. If they tried to keep track of every illegally occupied house in Edgartown, they wouldn't have time to do anything else. Besides, where would the college kids live if they didn't live in one of Ben's outhouses?"

"I know, I know. But it's disgusting."

Someone, maybe God, agreed with that assessment, because in early spring someone had torched one of Ben's houses and hadn't been caught yet. The year before, the same thing had happened to Ben's Oak Bluffs office. I didn't have any more idea than the cops did about who had burned the house, but as for the Oak Bluffs job, I attributed that to some in-town fire starter.

Oak Bluffs, one of the island's three biggest towns, which doesn't mean much in terms of population since only about twelve thousand people live on the whole island in the winter, is rightly famous for its Victorian gingerbread houses and its long-standing tradition of racial diversity, particularly as a summer resort for well-to-do Afro-Americans. As perhaps is unknown to its tourists and summer population, but is well known to year-round islanders, OB is also renowned for its hot-headed political factions. Typical small-town squabbles are squared or even cubed in Oak Bluffs, where no political decision is non-controversial and petty violence and vitriol are the norm: insults are exchanged in the newspapers and during town business meetings, cars of political figures are keyed and have their tires slashed and their windows broken, and occasionally someone gets a bloody nose.

Ben Krane, being at once a lawyer, a realtor, and the owner of some of the most disgraceful summer rentals on the island, naturally had his share of enemies, and in my view some OB citizen had torched his office for public or private reasons. In any case, Ben had not rebuilt in Oak Bluffs, but had reestablished his office in Edgartown, where tempers might run as high but actions were much more restrained. They don't burn people out in Edgartown, they chill them out.

Like the office fire, the blaze that later had leveled Ben's big old rotten rental house was very overtly a case of arson.

From Zee's point of view, the fire was just fine since no one had gotten hurt and Ben now had one less slum to rent out at exorbitant prices to summer kids. She wouldn't have minded if all such buildings burned down. It was a widely agreed-upon assessment. Ben Krane, rich and getting richer, was not a beloved figure with the local health board, the police, the neighbors of his decaying buildings, or the kids who rented his places, who were getting ripped off and knew it but didn't know what to do about it except trash the places when they left and leave them in even worse shape than they found them when they moved in. Ben publicly howled at their ingratitude and often refused to return the kids' security deposits, but never fixed anything up more than he absolutely had to before renting the place out again the next summer for even more money. And he didn't mind being a public outcast, either. He had money, and because he had money he had women and he didn't have to hang on to any of them longer than he wanted because there were always more.

It drove Zee wild and made her uncharacteristically sullen. "Why don't those women ever wise up?" she'd ask me when the news of Ben's latest ex-bedmate reached the streets.

"They're desperate," I'd explain. "They know I'm taken and it drives them to do mad things. They deserve sympathy, not impatience."

"I'm the one who deserves sympathy. I'm the one who lives with you!"

We got home in time to square away kids and gear, and to fillet our keeper bluefish and get them soaking in brine in preparation for smoking, before Warren Quick arrived with his load of lumber for my addition. He was driving his old truck with the logo on the door reading QUICK ERECTION COMPANY—WE GET IT UP FAST AND IT STAYS UP! Warren was a straight-arrow, West Coast guy who had apparently brought some California humor with him when he'd moved to the Vineyard and gotten his building business going in West Tisbury. I was surprised to see Susanna, his wife, riding in the cab with him.

He backed around the house to my lumber pile, climbed out, and the two of us began to unload. Susanna, babe on her hip and holding her eldest by the hand, went into the house, presumably to trade mom talk with Zee. Warren was quiet as usual. Unlike a lot of Californians, he never had much to say.

Before we got all of the lumber stacked, Zee came out the back door and waved me toward her. She had a frown on her face. I went to her.

"Come in," she said. "I want you to listen to Susanna. She's got a problem and she needs help."

"Serious?"

She flicked her eyes at Warren. "Serious enough. Somebody's writing her nasty letters."

I had quit the Boston PD because I was tired of trying to solve the dilemmas of the world and just wanted to be left alone. But woe is everywhere, of course, so I left Warren to finish the stacking and followed Zee into the house.

3

Susanna Quick was about thirty years old. She had an oval face with big blue eyes, light brown hair, a just-right nose, and full lips. Her hair was thick and her body was petite and nicely shaped. Warren's and her kids were just a tad younger than ours, and took after their mother in looks and coloring. The eldest, Abigail, who looked like Susanna, was going to give her parents a lot of grief in not too many more years; boys were going to be after her like hounds on a fox.

Susanna and Warren had arrived on the Vineyard with enough money to set up a business. He was good with his hands and tools and she was good in the office, and the Quick Erection Company was doing okay in spite of or maybe even because of its outlandish West Coast name. On building-happy Martha's Vineyard, there's plenty of business for construction outfits that can do their jobs right, and the Quicks sold not only lumber but other building materials too, and thus got business from the do-it-yourselfers like me.

I didn't know them well, having only met them as a customer, but they had always seemed to be happy together. When their kids arrived, Susanna just put a playpen in the office and kept on working. I admired her for that, being of similar inclination with regard to Josh and Diana; I liked having them around me.

Nurse Zee, who had met Susanna at the hospital, where all young Vineyard parents appear sooner or later for medical advice or assistance, had taken to her immediately, in part because they shared the drama of having young children about whom they had a lot to learn, and in part because Susanna was cheerful and full of life.

She didn't look so cheerful now.

"I'll take the kids outside so the two of you can talk without any little ears around," said Zee. She picked up the baby and reached for Abigail's hand.

"Let's go watch Warren unload lumber," said Zee to Josh and Diana, who were inside because everyone else was.

Zee and the four children went out. I looked at Susanna, who was sitting on the couch behind the coffee table that held the vise that held the lock that I practiced opening with the picks I'd gotten in an up-island yard sale. As far as I knew, I was the only apprentice lock picker in the neighborhood.

"Warren doesn't know about this," she said. "He wouldn't understand. He's so . . . pure."

"Understand what?" I sat down across from her.

Susanna twirled her thumbs.

"Zee says that you used to be a policeman."

"Yes. In Boston."

"She says I can trust you." Her blue eyes were deep and somber.

"I'm glad she thinks so."

Silence sat in the room while Susanna studied me. Then she made her decision.

"I've been getting phone calls. A man. He knows things I didn't think anyone knew. At least anyone here."

"Blackmail?"

"I'm not sure. Until yesterday he just made calls. He never said he wanted anything, he just told me what he knew. What he knows."

Everybody has secrets, so it was no surprise that Susanna had hers. I had mine, certainly. I hoped no one knew about some of them.

"What happened yesterday?"

She opened her purse and took out an envelope. "I got

this." She handed the envelope to me. Since there were probably dozens of fingerprints on it already, I took it. Inside was a folded piece of paper with a photograph printed on it. The picture was of a bondage scene featuring a bound and gagged woman wearing a mask, a cap with a feather, a cape, and a scanty green costume that looked vaguely as if it belonged in a Robin Hood movie. She was young and beautiful and was staring wide-eyed at a cloaked and hooded masked man dressed all in black. I thought I recognized the woman's eyes.

I handed the picture back to her. Compared with some of the stuff I'd seen, it was pretty mild.

"It's a printout from the Internet," said Susanna. "There's a lot of that sort of thing available, they tell me. In this one I was a superhero named Oriona. You know, it's a feminization of Orion the Hunter? She always hunted down the bad guys so she could capture them, but naturally she got captured instead and the villains got to humiliate and abuse her to their hearts' content. I made several Oriona films when I was eighteen or nineteen."

She looked at me as if trying to determine how I felt about such things.

"There's a market for it," I said.

She nodded. "Yes, although I didn't think much about the audience at the time. Don't get the wrong idea. The job paid pretty well, and nobody made me do it. I did it because I was young and was trying to get into the movies. I made myself into a blonde and called myself Eva L'Amour. It was actually fun most of the time, and I met some people I still like." She paused, and then went on. "Later, I did other stuff. Rougher stuff. Movies, stills, whatever. By the time I realized that I was never going to be a movie star, I'd made a lot of it. Then I met Warren.

"He was with a construction outfit that took on a job right next to where I was working that week. We ran into each other and got to talking. He wanted to start his own business, and I was ready to leave the gags and chains to somebody else. I never told him what I'd been doing, because he was so nice. We even go to church, you know. Every Sunday."

"Ah."

"So we got married in California and moved here, to Martha's Vineyard, where nobody knew me. His folks had died and left him some money and I'd squirreled away a nest egg of my own, so we were able to start up the business. Now this has happened."

Silence returned to the room.

"Has this man on the phone threatened you?" I asked finally.

"No. He just talks about Oriona, and how much he likes looking at her and knowing that Eva L'Amour is living right here on the Vineyard, where he can see her in person anytime he likes. He calls himself the Man in Black."

"Do you recognize the voice?"

"No. It's muffled. It scares me, though. He knows all about me." She wound her fingers together and then unwound them again. "If it was just me, or even just me and Warren, I wouldn't mind. But I've got Warren and the kids now and I don't want anything I did a long time ago to hurt them."

Let's talk about our families, class. What does your mom do, Abigail?

My mom is a porn queen.

"Here's what I think," I said. "You should contact the telephone company and tell them that you're getting harassing calls. Among other things, they have gadgets these days that you can put on your phone and that'll let you trace any call you get. Usually, when one of these heavy breathers gets himself identified, he stops making the calls right then and there."

She nodded. "That sounds good. I'll do that. Maybe that's all it'll take. I can't understand how this guy found out about me. My name is different, my hair is different, and I'm a lot older."

"It's a small world," I said. "People come to the Vineyard from all over, even from California. They wander everywhere these days. The stranger you talk to in China may live next to you on Nantucket." I put a smile on my face. "That's why you always have to be careful about what you say. The person you're insulting may be the sister of the person you're talking to."

She didn't smile back, so I offered another possibility. "I recognized you in the picture because of your eyes, even though Oriona was wearing a mask. You may have gotten older and moved and changed your name and the color of your hair, but your eyes haven't changed. Any fan of the pictures you made out west might recognize those eyes if he saw you now. It could be that your caller is a customer of your business and recognized you in your office."

Susanna frowned. "I don't like that idea at all!"

"And there was that picture of you and Warren at the church fair in the *Gazette* last spring. Maybe the guy saw that. It was a good shot of you. You do have eyes that are hard to forget. Was it just a little after that when you got the first telephone call?"

Susanna thought. "I guess it was. I never put the two together, but maybe I should have."

"Besides the phone company, you should go to the post office and to the police," I said. "They'll both help you."

She shook her head. "No. No police. I don't want any police. The police are like everybody else. They talk to their friends and the friends talk and pretty soon everybody in town will know. That's exactly what I don't want!"

"I think you can trust the cops," I said. "They deal with worse than this all the time and never tell anyone who doesn't need to know." It was true that cops know more about the dark side of everyday life than the rest of us: the wife beaters, the drunks, the predators and the prey, the vicious and the victims. It was also pretty true, but not completely true, that they usually don't talk about such things to civilians.

But Susanna was firm. "No. No police. And no post office, either. At least not right now. I'll talk with the phone people, though, and see if I can get one of those tracers for my phone." She twisted her hands. "I hope you understand. I just want to keep this as quiet as possible."

"Of course."

"Maybe I'll be able to identify this man right away."

"That would probably end your troubles with him."

"Yes." Her mind seemed far ahead of her mouth. She looked at me. "Will you help me?"

I was surprised. I'd thought the advice I'd given her was the help she'd come for.

"How?" I asked.

"If I find out who it is, I want you to talk to him." She glanced at the door. "I don't want Warren to know about this. You were a policeman. You know how to talk to these people. I want you to do it. Will you?"

There is no escaping the plague rats. They're always close by, even in Eden.

"If you find him, I'll talk to him," I said.

"Thank you." She gave a small smile. "I feel a lot better." She stood up. "I'll go save your wife from my children." She put out her hand.

"I haven't done anything yet." I held her hand for an extra heartbeat and said, "There's one thing you should keep in mind: When you turn over rocks, you sometimes find things you don't expect. If we do this, things may come to light that you might not anticipate or want to know."

"You and I will be the only ones who know it," she said. "I'm going to trust you."

As I followed her out into the yard, I thought of the old, familiar saying that two can keep a secret if one of them is dead.

4

I was more of a two-by-four carpenter than a cabinet-maker, but if I took my time I could make things fit. The key word was *time*. I needed more of it than a real carpenter would need, but I didn't have enough money to hire a pro to help, so the new wing to our house was progressing at a fairly sedate rate. My plan was to have it done by fishing derby time in September, so I was working at it pretty steadily. When I got it finished, not only would the kids have their own rooms, but the room they now shared would once more be available for our occasional guests, such as Brady Coyne and Quinn, who planned to come down and do some derby fishing.

Because Zee was back at work at the emergency ward of the hospital and thus was gone when she had the day shift, I often had the children to tend while I was working. Since many women, most, maybe, have to do their work with their children underfoot, I didn't feel any grounds for complaint, but I, like the moms, had to keep one eye on my offspring while I tended to other things.

Toward this end, I'd built a sort of corral for Diana in the backyard beside the addition I was putting up, so she wouldn't wander too far. Josh, being older, liked to help me with the building some of the time, so he got to be outside of the fence and wear his own little carpenter's apron and wield his minihammer when the notion took him. I sawed and hammered carefully when he was helping me, and when he tired of the building biz, I'd put him in with Diana and let them entertain themselves while I kept working.

As stay-at-home parents have always done, I sometimes wondered what miracles I might perform if I had a baby-sitter. On the other hand, as many of those other parents would probably also agree, I didn't want a baby-sitter tending my little ones all day. Even Mary Poppins would have been only a part-time employee at our place. I'd lived a long time without children, and I wanted to watch them grow up now that I had some.

So the new wing of the house went up slowly, as I stretched my money and split my attention between carpentry and kids.

Today, however, Zee was off work and was taking advantage of her free time to do some serious momming, so I was able to concentrate on construction. While I did, I thought about Susanna Quick and the computer-generated photo of her as Oriona in bondage.

I had encountered people in various forms of the sex industry when I was a cop in Boston and, after a period of surprise at the variety of activities that people would pay to do or have done to them, had finally concluded that there really was no such thing as abnormal sex. Every imaginable act was normal for a lot of people, it seemed, even though many such acts were illegal.

However, Zee and I were probably the last people in the United States without a computer, and I had never once even looked over anyone's shoulder at the famous Information Superhighway, so I had never observed computer-sex offerings. I had, of course, read about the controversies having to do with such material: the fears of some that morality, especially that of children, would be destroyed by exposure to graphic sexual images, and the fears, real or faked, of others that their constitutional rights would be eroded if any sort of censorship was imposed upon the medium.

My own view was that any sexual activity between consenting adults, barring sexually motivated murder-suicide, was okay with me. On the other hand, I did draw the line when it came to adults engaging in sexual acts with kids, because I didn't think that kids, especially young ones, really knew what was going on. And older ones didn't have the maturity to make sensible judgments. Of course, when I'd been on the Boston PD, I'd encountered some pretty childish adults and some pretty adult children, so just when a kid became old enough to be considered responsible for his or her sexual acts was a little elusive to me. I also had no notion at all whether exposure to explicit sexual images had any effect on the morality of children or anyone else.

So I wasn't offended by the notion that years back Susanna, like many a woman before her, had let herself be photographed doing things she later probably wished she hadn't done, or at least regretted having been filmed.

On the other hand, I wasn't persuaded that I had gotten all of the story, or surprised that I hadn't. Maybe there was still some cop in me, some expectation that people will lie when it suits their purposes: when they don't want something known, when they're afraid, when they're protecting someone. When this, when that. It's not uncommon for some to lie so much that they reach a point when they no longer realize that the lie isn't the truth. Hadn't Nietzsche commented that when our memory of having committed an ignoble act conflicts with our desire to believe that we are too honorable to have possibly committed the deed, memory always gives way to desire?

I grazed my thumb with my hammer, and for a while carefully put Susanna Quick out of my mind and concentrated on my carpentry. I wasn't so good at this kind of work that I could do it and think creatively about something else at the same time. I could do that while fishing and shellfishing, but not while house building.

No matter. It was none of my business anyway. If Susanna had a secret she wanted to keep from me, it was okay with me.

I hammered and measured and sawed and hammered

some more. The sweet smell of sawdust and wood filled my nostrils, and I worked steadily. Then I stopped, holding three nails in my teeth.

Susanna's secret was okay with me, unless the secret was a dangerous one and she was willing to risk me rather than her husband. If it was that sort of secret, I wanted to know about it before I met the mysterious Man in Black.

Maybe, for instance, he wasn't as mysterious as she had indicated. Maybe she knew who he was and what he wanted and didn't want Warren put in harm's way when she confronted him. Maybe she figured that what with me being a head taller and pounds heavier than Warren, and being an ex-cop, I was a better bet to deal with the guy than Warren was.

Maybe.

Maybe not.

Maybe I was imagining things.

Maybe Susanna was the Queen of Siam.

Was there still a Siam?

I didn't think so, but I'd lost track of a lot of countries quite a while back. Partly on purpose, since just keeping track of the little part of Martha's Vineyard that I lived on took up most of my time. So these days I not only tried to ignore the Big World, but I didn't even pay much attention to America, over on the other side of Vineyard Sound. In this respect, I was getting more and more like the *Vineyard Gazette*, that excellent newspaper that never took note of anything not having to do with the island. The *Gazette* wouldn't report on World War III unless someone from the Vineyard was involved.

I took a nail from my mouth and whacked it home, then whacked some more home and measured and sawed and hammered. Out beyond the garden I could see, between hacks and whacks, novice windsurfers learning their sport on the enclosed waters of Sengekontacket Pond. There, they could fall off and never have to worry about being blown out to sea. Beyond the pond, on the barrier

beach that carried the road between Edgartown and Oak
Bluffs, the cars that had been parked end to end all day
were heading home, where their passengers would soon
shower away sand and salt before cocktails and plans for
another lovely island evening. And beyond the beach, on
the dark blue water of Nantucket Sound, sailboats and
powerboats were coming into the harbor. Maybe Susanna's
Man in Black was wearing his black swimsuit while enjoying the beach or sitting at the tiller of his boat, looking aloft
at the set of his sails and planning on giving Susanna a call
this evening.

Could be.

"Hey," said Zee, coming around the corner of the
house. "Call it a day and go get Corrie so we'll have time
for drinks before supper."

I didn't need a second invitation. I stashed my tools,
sloshed off the afternoon's grime in the outdoor shower,
and put on clean clothes. I found Zee and gave her a kiss.

"I'll be right back."

"I figure grilled bluefish and veggies for supper."

"A winner plan."

"I'll get the grill going while you're gone and chop the
veggies."

"Excellent. A woman's place is in the kitchen."

"No one has ever figured out where men belong!"

"Anywhere you are, sweets, is the place for me."

"How about when I'm cleaning the bathroom?"

"Well, almost anywhere. I'd be there, too, but it just
drives me crazy that women insist on leaving the toilet
seat down!"

I got into my rusty Land Cruiser and drove to the
house where Corrie was staying. Zee's little Jeep was
newer and more stylish, but the Toyota and I were old
companions and I drove it when I had a choice.

Corrie was sitting on the steps of the sagging porch
with his guitar case at hand. Again I was conscious of illness in his face. Beside him was a frowning college-age

boy. As I stopped, Corrie got up and motioned the boy to follow him over to the car.

"J.W.," he said, "this is Adam Washington. Adam's the grandson of my pal Ernie Washington, and the guy who's putting me up. Adam, this is J. W. Jackson, the fella I've been telling you about."

I put out my hand and Adam Washington took it briefly.

"Hello," I said.

"Hello," he said.

No sparks of immediate friendship leaped between us. Adam's expression of discontent had not left his face. He stepped back, and Corrie got into the truck. Corrie looked out at him. "You come by the coffeehouse later if you want to hear me bang this here box." He slapped the guitar case.

"Yeah," said Adam, stepping farther back. "Sure. I'll try to get up there. See you later."

I drove away.

"Everybody's got troubles," said Corrie after a while. He sighed.

"Or at least they think they have," I said, remembering Susanna's complaints. It had been my experience that we create a lot of our griefs out of whole cloth.

"Oh, there's make-believe problems, sure enough," said Corrie, "but there's real ones too. That boy acts like he's got his share."

"Which kind?"

"Can't say," said Corrie. "I'm too old for him to talk to. He's unhappy about something, though. Woman, maybe?"

I glanced at him. He was sliding a pill into his mouth and slipping the plastic vial back into his shirt pocket. His face was impenetrable.

5

At our house, Zee took Corrie by the arm. "Jeff will tend the grill while you and I have a drink and yak. Come inside and tell us what you'd like."

Corrie would like a beer. I went into the kitchen, poured vodka on the rocks (with two black olives) for Zee, and got a Sam Adams for Corrie and another for me. When I came back, he was looking around the living room approvingly. "Still got the rods hanging on the ceiling, like you said. I don't remember that stove. Used to be just the fireplace."

"I put the stove in to make the place more civilized for my blushing bride," I said. "It's a more efficient heat source. I traded some work for it."

He nodded. "The barter system is best for them with no money. I see you still got your daddy's decoys. That man could surely carve."

"It's a talent I didn't inherit, so we show off the ones he made."

Oliver Underfoot and Velcro, the family cats, rubbed against Corrie's ankles and got scratched ears in return. Instant friendship. Corrie straightened, glanced at the lock and picks I kept on the coffee table in front of the couch, smiled, and moved to the fireplace mantel, where we kept Zee's expanding collection of trophies.

"Well, well, I see that you're a competitive pistol shooter, ma'am. I don't believe I've ever met another lady who does that."

"Just call me Jessica James," said Zee with a smile. "Yes, I shoot. It's fun."

"She's a natural, according to Manny Fonseca," I said. "She's better than I ever was, for sure."

"Maybe that's because I'm only shooting at targets," said Zee. "When Jeff was shooting a pistol, people were shooting back."

Pretty effectively, too. I had the bullet scars to prove it. Another reason for giving up police work and living the fisherman's life.

"Never was much of a shootist, myself," said Corrie. "I did some hunting when I was a boy, but since then,I ain't had much time for guns. Some of the people I've known down through the years had a different view, of course." He laughed. "What I get for hanging around saloons and nightclubs all my life. Lucky for me that those pistol packers mostly liked my music, otherwise I might have some holes in my old Martin and in me, too!"

"Well, our guns are all locked up, so there'll be no shooting out the lights this evening," said Zee. "Come on, let's go up onto the balcony and talk while Jeff looks after the children and gets started on supper. I may be a better shot than he is, but he's a better cook than I am. You kids stay down here with your pa, but don't get too near the grill."

"A man should know how to feed himself," said Corrie, following her to the stairs. "I make no claims to being a chef, but I can bake a fish and use a frying pan if I need to. I've lived a long time, and I ain't starved yet!"

The cats and kids trailed me into the kitchen, where I collected the mesquite-marinated bluefish and chopped vegetables, and they stayed with me as I went outside to the gas grill, which was going nicely.

Zee had chopped, sliced, and marinated onions, peppers, precooked potatoes, and some other dibs and dabs of veggies from the fridge. I had more time than I needed, so I put all of the food on the table of the grill, and ran around in the yard for a while with Joshua and Diana.

Just running around was a good kids' game. Our two

laughed and screamed a lot, which was the main point, and there weren't any rules except getting caught every now and then, and getting away other times. First, one of us was the chaser and catcher and then another one was. We also did a lot of falling down just as we were about to escape or catch somebody. From the balcony, Zee and Corrie watched and talked, like spectators at an arena game.

When I figured it was time to get to cooking, I fell down one last time and let both kids fall on top of me so we could all catch our breath, then got up and walked the three of us around the house a few times to quiet us down some more. On the last circumnavigation, I informed the audience in the balcony that dinner would soon be served, then shooed Joshua and Diana away from the grill and went to work on supper.

As is often the case with good food, there wasn't much to cooking this meal, especially since the prep work had already been done. I dumped the veggies into the perforated metal wok, put the wok on one side of the grill, and laid the bluefish fillets on the other. I spent five minutes stirring and turning the vegetables as they roasted, then turned the fish and stirred the veggies for another five minutes, and that was that. I turned off the grill and carried everything into the house, where I sliced up some homemade white bread and popped the cork from the jug of the house white—sauvignon blanc.

We ate on the porch, and everything was delish!

"My, my," said Corrie, pushing back his plate and touching his napkin to his lips. "I don't remember a finer meal. You folks know how to live."

"It's hard to beat fresh bluefish and veggies," agreed Zee. "You'll have to eat with us again while you're down here."

"You say that one more time and I'll be the man who came to dinner and never left." He looked approvingly at Joshua and Diana, who were seated across from him. "I'm glad to see your little ones eat big-people food. Some kids are pretty picky."

"They inherited my genes," grinned Zee. "There's nothing I won't eat a ton of!"

"I may be an old man," said Corrie, digging a hand into the pocket of his jacket, "but I still got an eye for the ladies, so you can take my word for it when I tell you that you don't look like some other women I know who love their food. I don't see any sign of that ton." His hand came out holding a pipe. "You folks mind if I step outside for a smoke? I got a habit that I just can't shake."

"You smoke right here," said Zee. "Jeff smoked a pipe for years and still has his rack of briars and corncobs that he can't throw away because he may start again anytime. And I like the smell of a pipe, myself, so you just light up!" She stood and started collecting plates and silverware. "Stay right where you are," she said to Corrie as he started to stand. "It's the way we do it: if I cook, Jeff cleans; if he cooks, I clean. Division of labor and all that. You're a guest, so you don't get to help."

"I'll get the brandy and *biscotti*, then." I got up and did that, and when the table was cleared we all sipped and ate, enjoying Corrie's pipe as we did.

Joshua and Diana stayed with the grown-ups and, after a bit, Corrie reached out a long arm and pulled a shiny penny from behind Diana's ear. "Well, look what I found," he said. "Don't you wash behind your ears, young lady?"

Joshua, who hadn't known that his sister kept pennies behind her ears, was impressed even more when Corrie found another new penny behind *his* ear. Then Corrie found one in midair. All told, he found ten brand-new pennies in ten unexpected places and gave five to each small Jackson.

"How do you do that?" asked a very interested Joshua.

"Magic," explained Corrie.

There was still some light when a Jeep came down our driveway, bringing one of the Skye twins to baby-sit. Jill and Jen Skye were the teenage daughters of our friends John and Mattie Skye, and looked so much alike that I never knew which one I was talking to. But they both loved Joshua and Diana and both were at the top of our list of sitters.

The Jeep stopped and a twin got out.

"Hi, Jen," said Zee, saving me the usual confusion about which sister I was dealing with. "Come and meet Corrie Appleyard."

"Hi," said Jen to Corrie as they shook hands. "Zee told me why she needed a baby-sitter tonight, and my dad and mom were pretty excited when I told them that you were here on the island. I think they're going to be there at the Moon Cusser."

"I'll look forward to meeting them," said Corrie in his courtly manner, as Joshua and Diana, who liked Jen as much as she liked them, crowded around her.

"Perfect timing," said Zee, looking at her watch. "Let's head for Vineyard Haven."

The original Moon Cusser had been in Oak Bluffs, and for a while, back in the roaring sixties, had been a busy and successful place, certainly the island's finest coffee-house. My father took me there a few times when I was little, so I could hear the folk performers who came to play their instruments and sing. The only ones I could remember were Ian and Sylvia, whose voices and harmonies I still had on some ancient, well-worn 33's, but there had been many other performers, all part of the blossoming revival of folk music, which for a time had been a powerful alternative to rock and roll.

The Moon Cusser II was in Vineyard Haven, and in this later age, when traditional, mostly acoustic music was not in strong favor with the younger crowd which spent millions at concerts and on disks and tapes, it still hung on, serving coffee and featuring musicians sometimes unknown to the fans of the latest musical fad. Always on the verge of going under, the café was a small miracle of its own kind. It was the sort of place that you might expect to find a man like Corrie Appleyard.

The current Cusser was located in a battered building near the infamous Five Corners of Vineyard Haven, which is arguably the site of the worst traffic jams on Martha's Vineyard (although others will spiritedly contend that the A & P–Al's Package Store jam in Edgartown deserves the championship). The Cusser's single room was small, clean, furnished with worn chairs and tables, its walls and ceiling decorated with posters and pictures of musicians. The coffee bar was against the far wall, and the small stage with its single mike was in a back corner.

When we came in, there was already quite a crowd, relatively speaking, since a full house was a rarity at the Cusser. People looked up from their cups when we entered, and several straightened and then leaned over and whispered in their companions' ears as they spotted Corrie's guitar case.

There was a "Reserved" card on a table next to the stage, and Corrie led us there.

"A perk for the performer," said Corrie in an almost whisper. "I called this afternoon and told them some friends would be with me and I wanted them close."

We sat, and a waitress wearing shorts, sandals, and a T-shirt was instantly there to take our orders. When she left, Aldo came over. Aldo ran the place. He shook hands all around.

"Glad you could make it," he said. He glanced around the room. More people were coming in. "Good house tonight. You've still got a lot of fans here, Corrie."

"Good to see them," said Corrie.

"Well, any time you're ready, then."

Aldo walked back to the bar.

Across the room I saw Mattie and John Skye and their other twin sit down at a table. They saw us and waved and smiled.

"I reckon I better get at it," said Corrie. "Talk with you folks later."

He stepped up onto the stage, opened his guitar case,

and brought out an ancient Martin flattop. I was pleased and surprised to note that it was the same model as the one that had belonged to my father and now belonged to me. Corrie touched the strings, adjusted one that already sounded fine to me, and began to play. Although my guitar was the same as his, mine had never produced such fine sound. It was more than note and tone; it rose from the void and imposed order on chaos. Then Corrie began to sing, and his voice was like an ancient boat on deep waters, carrying his listeners through darkness toward light.

— 6 —

Corrie's fingers caressed the strings of the old Martin and his voice melted into the sound of the guitar until I heard them as only one instrument. It produced classic blues sometimes and other music other times, but always it spoke of old and timeless truths. It wasn't a loud sound, but it was strong and haunting and it quieted the room. It told of sorrow, of stony roads and bruised feet, of betrayal and mourning. But it was more than a lament; it went past lamenting toward freedom; it was music out of the experience of black Americans, but it belonged to everyone everywhere. When Corrie finished his first set, the applause was almost apologetic.

He came to our table and sat down. I had coffee waiting for him.

"Great," said Zee, smiling. I nodded.

John Skye crossed the room and put out a hand, which Corrie took. "Mighty fine," said John. "Takes me back to when I heard you and Josh White in the fifties."

"Long time ago," said Corrie.

"You're better than ever. Did B. B. King learn that last number from you, or did you learn it from him?"

Corrie grinned. "We both got it from another guy."

John straightened. "I'll leave you alone. It's been a pleasure to meet you." He went back to his table.

"Our baby-sitter's dad," said Zee.

"Ah. Nice fellow."

"He's a professor up at Weststock College," I said. "Teaches medieval lit."

Corrie laughed. "Probably explains why he likes my music. It's pretty old, too." He looked around the room, and most of the smile faded from his face. "Guess Adam didn't make it. There's a few young folks still playing and singing the blues, but most of them are listening to other kinds of music these days."

"When the new stuff is gone, the blues will still be around," said Zee, who, like me, was not a fan of most popular music. "Who's Adam?"

"Grandson of a friend. The boy I'm staying with. Thought he might come by tonight, but I guess not."

"His loss," said Zee, wasting no sympathy on Adam. She patted Corrie's hand with hers.

"You ever decide to go on the road, and if I have any money, I'll hire you to do my publicity," said Corrie, a new smile appearing on his face.

From beyond the walls of the building we could hear the sounds of traffic and, somewhere far off, that of a siren. Some cop was heading for an accident, or an ambulance was taking somebody to the hospital, or a fire truck was on its way. The island was not immune to blues of its own.

"I better get back up there," said Corrie.

He returned to the mike and, as the audience quieted, began a second set, this time alternating songs of many kinds: soulful ones, sad ones, comic ones that startled the audience into laughter, gospel songs, songs I remembered from my childhood, followed by others I'd never heard. The sounds of the outer world went away as his fingers picked and stroked the strings of the old Martin, and his ageless voice filled the room like smoke.

> Saturday night at Kenney's,
> We were sitting in a booth;
> Tom Blues walked in among us,
> Looking tear stained and uncouth.

Tom says, "Gimme a drink of whiskey,
Gimme a drink of gin;
I'm feeling mighty thirsty,
Though I know that it's a sin."

Corrie let the guitar speak alone for a while, then came back to the words of the song.

"It's not that I'm a bitcher, boys;
I always wear a smile;
but when I'm feeling low down,
I got to go on down town,
Just to lose those Down Town Tom Tom Blues."

Drinking liquor to forget hard times. A traditional cure that rarely worked, but one a lot of us had tried, for we all want to lose the blues at some time or other. I wished Tom well, whoever he might be.

Corrie sang three sets before casing the guitar and stepping off the stage for the final time. Looking weary. The audience filed out, many of them coming by the table to greet and thank him before they left. Mattie and John Skye pulled up chairs and sat down with us. Aldo shut the door behind the last of the others and got a bottle and glasses from under the bar.

"One for the road?"

"You bet."

He poured and we drank. I felt good.

"Never heard that Tom Blues song before," said John.

"Got it from a fella named Charlie Miller out in Gunnison, Colorado," said Corrie. "Lot of good songs floating around one place or another. I like to learn as many as I can."

"It's been a fine night," said Aldo. "Be glad to have you back again sometime."

Corrie nodded. "Be glad to come."

"We'll work it out, then. A lot of folks living on this little island appreciate good music. It's what keeps me open."

Aldo was right about the island's music fans. There were a lot of them. The Vineyard had more than its share of music makers, too. All kinds, ranging from people playing in rock bands to members of baroque and classical groups. Soloists, too, who could play almost any instrument you could name, and who sang in languages from all over the world. Some of them were famous, but others lived quietly, known only to year-round islanders, and performing only for friends or small groups of local aficionados.

When the island's renowned summer colony of movie and television stars, politicians, writers, musicians, and artists left in the fall, these year-round people, and other equally talented artists, scholars, and writers hidden away in the villages and woods, stayed where they were. They, like the far beaches and other secret spots rarely seen by the summer tourists, were, to me, the better part of the Vineyard's charm. Because of them, I rarely felt a need to leave the island in search of culture. If I wanted a taste of art or literature, I could find it right here, minding its own business.

Zee glanced at her watch and pushed back her chair. "It's save-the-baby-sitter time, folks."

We went out into the night. Vineyard Haven is a dry town, so there were no bars emptying out, no noisy revelers in the streets, such as might be found in Edgartown or Oak Bluffs, where booze could be bought and sold and where, as a consequence, most of the island's fights could be observed. With no ferries arriving this late, the infamous Five Corners was as free of traffic as the sidewalks were free of barflies, so we got to the Land Cruiser without meeting another soul, and headed for Corrie's house under the star-spangled sky.

You couldn't see things as well as you could in the daylight, but there was no mistaking a Ben Krane house, even in the middle of the night.

"What a bloodsucker." Zee's voice was nearly a snarl.

Cars lined the dirt road in front of the house and jammed the yard, and it seemed that every light in the place was on. The door was open and we could see young men and women standing on the sagging porch drinking beer, talking, and waving their arms. Over them, under them, around them, and through them blared the throbbing music the younger generation loved as much as I disliked it. Obviously it was party time. I double-parked the truck and Corrie studied the porch.

"Whole lot of socializing going on," he said. "Well, thanks for the ride."

He opened the door and stepped out. The sound of the music and voices poured in with the faint fragrance of grass. The word *fire* reached my ears through the hubbub of voices and the pounding music, but I didn't see any sign that they had a grill. Some faces turned toward us, maybe wondering who we were, then turned away again.

"Thanks for the fishing, the meal, and the ride," said Corrie.

"And thank you for the music," said Zee. "It's been a while since we've been in a church, but you'll probably see us there when you play."

"Hey, Corrie," said a voice. A young man materialized beside him and peered into the truck. The look of expectation on his face turned instantly to disappointment. "Oh," he said. "Sorry." He straightened and looked at Corrie. "I thought Adam might be with you. He said he might go to the coffeehouse."

"He might have started there but he didn't make it," said Corrie.

"Damn," said the young man. "That means he probably went after Millie." He frowned.

Corrie smiled. "I know that young woman. If I had a choice between spending time with her or listening to music I didn't know nothing about, I'd go to Millie, sure enough."

"Yeah," said the boy, "but I guess you haven't heard about the fire. The house where she lives burned down tonight, and we don't know if she was there or not. Everybody else who lived there was right here at the party when the fire started."

I remembered the siren. "Their house burned down and they're here at a party?"

He looked annoyed. "No! They were here when it started. Now they're back there watching their place and all their stuff go up in smoke." He waved at the noisy house. "These are other people from other houses. We have a scanner. We heard about the fire and we all tried to get to the house to help get stuff out, but the cops wouldn't let us near, so there was nothing we could do, and we came back here." He looked worried. "I wish Adam would call or something."

I would have been worried, too.

"He'll show up," said Corrie, frowning and putting a hand to his chest. "He's probably making up with Millie some place."

"Yeah, probably." The young man didn't look persuaded. "Well, I guess all we can do is wait." He turned and walked through the river of music that was pounding at us.

Corrie, still frowning, peered in at us again. "I'll see you folks again." He shut the car door and followed the young man toward the throbbing house.

"These kids had better worry about their own place going up in smoke," said Zee, frowning as I backed and turned. "It looks like a tinderbox!"

I had used the same term not long before, but in fact I had never seen a real tinderbox, and I doubted whether I knew anybody who had, outside of a museum; but Zee's point was sound: Vineyard slumlords, like their mainland ilk, were not famous for the safety features in their rental houses. The wonder was that more of the places didn't burn down before they fell down.

At home we found the Skye twin watching the late show on our tiny black-and-white television set, which had arrived at my previously TV-less house when Zee had moved in. It was part of her dowry, she had explained. We still didn't have a color set, but at least we had a set, such as it was.

"No problems here," said the twin, gathering up her possessions and getting her money. "How was the concert?"

"Sad and blue and funny sometimes," said Zee. "Corrie Appleyard is terrific. Your folks were there and they'll tell you all about it."

"The blues," said the twin. "I sing them myself, sometimes."

The twin said good night and left, and we went into the children's room to check on the darlings. They were asleep and looked quite angelic. We adjusted a blanket or two, the way parents do, and went to our own bed. We read our bedside-table books for a while, then turned out the light. Zee threw a long leg over mine and snugged in close.

"I love you," she said.

I pulled her against me. "Me, too."

"I had a good time tonight."

"Me, too."

"I hope nobody got hurt in the fire."

"Me, too."

I thought about the fire and the blues and Corrie's frown. Maybe somebody would write a song about a house burning down. Somebody probably already had. Winners may write the history books, but losers write the songs.

I heard the news at the Dock Street Coffee Shop, where the Jacksons were having breakfast: juice for everybody; coffee for the big people; cereal for Diana; toast, bacon, and a scrambled egg for Joshua, who didn't care for soft egg yolks; a bagel for Zee; and the full-bloat breakfast—sausage, eggs, toast, and fried potatoes—for me. Delish! And with your food, you got to watch the cook do his work, never wasting a motion, his arms as graceful as a hula dancer's, rhythmic as a symphony conductor's. And you got the latest gossip. What more could you ask? Today the talk was mostly about last night's fire.

Opinions ranged from the mild to the wild: Another damned Ben Krane firetrap! Be a good thing if every slum he owned burned down! Just lucky that nobody got hurt. But maybe somebody did. A girl was missing. Girl named Millicent Dowling, according to a cop somebody knew. Her friends called her Millie, and nobody had seen her since the fire. As soon as they got the ruins cooled down enough to make a search, the firemen would go in and see if she maybe didn't get out, or look for anybody else who might be in there. Fire marshals would have to figure out what started it, too.

"What do you think, J.W.? Arson or just an accident?"

I looked at Charlie Bensen. I was sitting between him and Joshua. Charlie liked fires and kept his scanner on all the time so he could go watch the firemen do their work. He'd been a volunteer himself until he got too old.

"I don't know, Charlie," I said. "You didn't do it, did you?"

Charlie grinned, showing a good set of new dentures. "I know what they say about firebugs working as firemen, but no, it wasn't me." He sobered. "Thing is, there was that arson last spring. 'Nother Krane place. Maybe somebody's got it in for Ben Krane."

"Maybe so."

Charlie chewed some toast. "You remember about twenty-five years back we had that string of arsons in town? Summer places, mostly, empty and usually off someplace where there wasn't a hydrant anyplace close. I worked on most of them fires, but we couldn't save many of the places. Us and the cops could never prove who did it, but finally the arson stopped. You remember that?"

I'd been about fifteen at the time, but I did remember it. The fires had spooked a lot of people. I nodded. "The story I got was that the cops had a pretty good idea who did it even though they couldn't prove anything, so they had a talk with the perp and he shut himself down."

"Yeah," said Charlie. "That was the scuttlebutt. I never heard who they had in mind. Say, maybe whoever it was is back at work and is torching Ben Krane's places because he knows nobody'll be too mad at him for doing it!" He gave me another grin.

"Plenty of people got it in for Ben Krane," said a voice from up the counter. That would be Zack Delwood, who didn't like anybody too much. Zack and I didn't socialize a lot.

I'd never thought that Zack was too bright, but he and Charlie were both right about Ben Krane. A lot of people would be glad if Ben got put out of business.

I, for instance, would not have wept if Ben had decided to move off island and take his houses and their occupants with him.

As if reading my mind, Zack loudly added, "Too damned

many college kids down here, too! Burn down all of Krane's damned houses and they'd have to stay home and leave us islanders alone!"

It was a variation on the ever-popular attack on the Vineyard's summer visitors. Locals who didn't own businesses moaned all season about the traffic and the crowds and how great it had been in the old days when you knew your neighbors and could find a parking spot on Main Street. The island's businesspeople, on the other hand, wanted all of the visitors they could get, because tourism greased the Vineyard's wheels. Zack, being of the first class, scorned the summer people. Of course, he scorned most islanders, too, being a mean-minded guy in general. He and I had a truce, however, so he usually left me and mine out of his wide-ranging condemnations of his fellow humans. I never could understand how anyone could be so sour, but Zack managed it.

"Zack's right about Ben and about them college students, too," said old Charlie, nodding his bald head. "We'd be better off without any of 'em. But I don't like the idea of burning buildings down when there's people in 'em."

"What are you talking about, Charlie?" said yet another voice. "You haven't missed a fire in forty years."

Charlie leaned forward and looked up the counter toward whoever it was that had made that crack. "I admit it. I do like to watch a fire, but I don't want no people inside of it! You want to burn down Ben Krane's houses, you do it in the wintertime when they're empty!"

"You burn 'em down, Charlie. You were the fireman, I never was! Haw! Haw!"

Had the speaker remembered *Fahrenheit 451* and its fire-starting firemen?

Charlie hadn't. "Only fires I ever started was in a stove, goddammit!"

Other voices entered in.

"Probably nobody started this one either. Probably bad

wiring. Ben Krane never puts a cent into those hovels of his."

"Or one of those college students got stoned and left a cigarette butt burning in a couch or something."

"How about them Sox?" asked someone, just to change the subject.

"What do you mean, how about 'em?" rejoined another fan. "It's only June, for God's sake. Plenty of time for them to do the Fenway flop."

"Hey," said Zee, who was always ready to talk baseball, "they may not have Roger anymore, but they have Pedro and they finally have an infield and some D in the outfield, too. They can catch anything hit near them. They'll be okay this year."

"They can't hit the long ball. You got to hit the long ball to win at Fenway."

Zee shook her head. "They hit the long ball for eighty years and never won a World Series. D is what wins for you. Same as in any sport. Ask the pros."

And so it went. Baseball, summer tourists, fishing, and the fire took turns occupying the attention of the talkers. Tragic, comic, and inane subjects in a typical human mix. I'd heard it all before, except for the part about Millicent Dowling. Millie. The girl Adam Washington had fought with and then had perhaps gone to find.

"I think we're done here," said Zee, wiping little hands and faces with napkins. "You kids ready to go?"

They were, and so we left, walking out into the parking lot at the foot of Main Street, where, it being early, there were actually still some parking slots.

Mike Smith's pickup was parked in front of the yacht club, which meant that Mike was already at work there, doing whatever needed to be done to keep the place shipshape and functioning, and in the channel beyond the club an early traveling yawl was heading out to sea. Off to our right, among the other moored boats this side of the

Reading Room, we could see the *Shirley J.,* our eighteen-foot Herrischoff *America* catboat, bobbing at her stake, her bow toward the small southwest wind that was slowly rising with the sun. Beyond her, in the still not too full harbor, other yachts, both sailboats and power, hung quiet and dewy at their moorings. In another few weeks, the harbor would be wall to wall with boats, but right now many of the moorings were empty.

Above us the pale blue sky arched toward the horizon, and around us the village was slowly coming to life. Edgartown, with its flowers, trees, and green lawns, its narrow streets and white- or gray-shingled houses, and its docks, boats, and blue harbor, is the Vineyard's loveliest town and not a place to make you think of smoking ruins or missing girls. Its great captains' houses, its famous pagoda tree (brought to America in a flowerpot by a long-ago seaman), its church towers, its lighthouse, its shops, and its beaches are almost make-believe in their beauty, and make it easy to understand why tens of thousands of tourists show up every year.

We too never tired of the village, although we stayed away from it as much as possible in the summer because of the crowds. In the early mornings, before many people were up and around, we'd sometimes come down to the coffee shop for breakfast, but once people got to stirring and the streets started filling up, we stayed at home or headed for the far beaches of Chappaquiddick, where the only tourists were fisherpeople or picnickers.

Unless we wanted to go for a day sail.

In that case we sneaked down Cooke Street to Collins Beach, where we kept our dinghy chained to the Reading Room dock to prevent it from being stolen by gentlemen yachtsmen who felt no moral inhibitions about taking other people's dinghies if they needed to get out to their boats after late-night drinking. From Collins we would row out to the *Shirley J.,* trade dinghy for catboat on the mooring line, and catch the wind for a sail down harbor or out past the lighthouse into Nantucket Sound.

Now, Zee, holding Diana's hand, was eyeing the *Shirley J.* speculatively. "What do you think?" she asked. "It's a nice wind."

"I think yes," I said. "How about down to the far corner of Katama? We can do some clamming while we sop up the beneficial rays of the sun, and tomorrow I'll fry up some of the catch and make a chowder with the rest."

Her white teeth flashed. "Let's do it. Home to get some gear and food, then back again."

One of the nice things about living on an island is that you can go sailing and clamming whenever you feel like it. We felt like it pretty often.

So it wasn't long before I was rowing us out to the stake, and not much later that we were beating down harbor, against both wind and falling tide, under the warming sun. We passed the huge house owned by the Vineyard's most famous car dealer, a guy who could fit our whole house in his living room, and then sailed by the lovely ketch *Wynjie,* admiring her as always as she swung at her mooring. In the lee of the hills to our right, we battled through the narrows into Katama Bay, caught the wind again, and headed on to the southeast corner of the bay. There I put our bow on the beach, dropped sail, unloaded family and gear, then pushed the boat back into the channel and dropped the hook.

The water was warm and the clam flats had risen out of the falling tide. We got the umbrella and the beach chairs set up, set the cooler near at hand, and got the beach blanket and the shovels and pails laid out. Zee stripped to her bikini, and I felt my eyes widen as usual. She saw my face and grinned. I helped the kids out of their shirts and turned them loose, since in that corner of Katama Pond the water is so shallow near the shore that it's a safe place for small children.

Another good thing about it is that it's one of the best spots in Edgartown for steamers and quahogs. Today I was after steamers, so I got my gloves and wire bucket and walked out onto the flats. Joshua came, too, wearing his own little rubber gloves.

There are a lot of ways to get steamer clams. You can dig for them with a shovel or a fork, you can use a toilet plunger to suck them up to the top of the sand, or, if you're a professional, you can use a pump and a hose to wash them up to where you can get to them with a rake.

I prefer to get down on my hands and knees and dig for them as if I were strip-mining. I don't own a pump-and-hose unit, and I think I break fewer shells with my hands than when I use a shovel or a fork. But you can slice your hands up pretty well when you're digging for clams, so good gloves make the job a lot easier. Joshua, wanting to do things the way his pa did, was also a digger, although his staying power wasn't as great as mine.

I liked to clam. There was a nice mindless quality about it. You could clam and enjoy the sun on your back and think about something else entirely.

In spite of my own wishes to stay away from grief, I thought about house fires and Millie Dowling and Adam Washington. Then I thought about Susanna Quick and her telephone calls. Once again the serpents in Eden seemed to be sliding out from under the rocks. Or maybe they were always out in the open, but I was just too blinded by the garden to see them.

— 8 —

At home again, I put my catch into a five-gallon bucket of salt water, so the clams could spit out sand overnight and be clean and ready to eat tomorrow. I put the bucket in the shade and got back to work on the addition to the house. Fires might burn, people might go missing, comets might come out of heaven and threaten the earth itself, but the world kept turning and all the normal stuff had to go on. It was another beautiful Vineyard day on beautiful Martha's Vineyard; no wonder I had no intention of living anywhere else.

Zee had Diana out in front of the house someplace, but Joshua was helping me, handing me nails that I dropped and steadying boards that I sawed and nailed. Maybe he'd end up with the magic hands that I lacked, hands that could do finish carpentry, hands that could fix a car or a radio, or build a boat, or carve a decoy, or play good blues or flamenco guitar, or do other subtle work that mine were not too good at. I hoped so.

I worked on and finally Joshua grew tired of playing grown-up, said, "Bye, Pa," and went off to join his mother and sister. Smart Joshua. Time enough later to be an adult, to wake to the farm forever fled. Time now to be young and easy, happy as the grass was green.

Green became red and my mind turned to last night's fire. Had Adam Washington ever showed up? Had Millie Dowling made an appearance, or were her ashes going to be found in the smoldering ruin of the house?

What a nosy person I was. Hadn't I moved down to the

island precisely because I wanted to be left alone and have no more to do with the troubles of the world? And wasn't it a fact that I'd only met Adam Washington once and I'd never met Millicent Dowling at all? That their fates were not my concern?

Yet the two of them occupied my thoughts. Corrie would be worried about his friend's son. Maybe that made it my concern.

I nailed another board and stepped back to admire my work. Not bad. At this rate, if I could come up with some money for materials, I'd have the new wing ready on schedule. That being the case, it seemed a good time to take a break and do something else.

Maybe take a ride over to the place where Corrie was staying and catch up on the news.

I put away my tools and went around the house to tell Zee my plans. No Zee. I went inside. She was in the kitchen holding Diana on her hip and stirring a pot of what smelled like cream of refrigerator soup, one of my favorites. Joshua was playing some sort of game with the cats, Oliver Underfoot and Velcro, which the three of them perfectly understood.

"We'll all go," Zee said, turning off the burner and shoving the pot to the back of the stove. She looked up at me. "I'm curious, too. What a pair we are."

I gave her a kiss. I liked her as much as I loved her. I got hold of Joshua and we all climbed into the Land Cruiser.

The house where Corrie was staying looked worse in the daylight than in darkness, and worse this morning than usual, since the lawn and porch were littered with the remains of last night's party: beer cans, empty bottles, crumpled potato chip bags, and other debris, including a T-shirt and what looked a lot like a pair of women's underpants. The place smelled of stale beer, sweat, and, faintly, marijuana. A beer keg lay beside the stairs to the porch.

Off to one side of the house, Corrie Appleyard was

squatting beside a battered moped, adjusting something. He glanced up, rose, and came toward us. He looked as though he hadn't slept too well. Apparently a life of late-night gigs had not immunized him to chaos or allowed him to ignore loud music and drunks and to snooze soundly through a Vineyard college party such as had happened here last night.

"Sleep well?" I asked.

He shrugged. "I've done better." He gestured toward the moped. "Had me a motorcycle once. That machine there belongs to my host, Adam. Should start a little easier now, but it still needs work."

Mopeds are one of the island's principal summer hazards, primarily because the people who rent them don't know how to ride them safely and are constantly crashing and being taken to the hospital in an ongoing drama known to the police as Moped Mop Up. Some of the more experienced police officers prefer night duty to day duty during the summer precisely because Moped Mop Up takes place for the most part during daylight hours, and they'd rather leave the scraping up and the hospital runs to the summer cops.

I looked at the rubble on the lawn. "If you slept at all last night, you're a better man than I am, Gunga Din."

He nodded. "You work some places I've worked, you could sleep through hell afterwards." He seemed in a good mood.

Zee apparently noted this. "Adam get back?"

He nodded. "Yes, ma'am. Late. After you all left."

So far, so good. "He ever catch up with the girl?" I asked.

Corrie smiled. "I heard him come home with a girl. I guess it was Millie, but I didn't see her." He nodded toward the house behind him. "They're all still sawing wood. Young folks these days ain't much on rising early."

Were they ever? I was glad that Millicent Dowling was okay and said so.

"Me, too," said Corrie, losing his smile. "Place where she lived was empty when it burned, but for a while people were afraid she was in it."

"Where was she?"

"Nobody has told me that yet."

Zee touched my sleeve. "Let's go have a look at the place. Maybe the fire marshal will be there and we can find out what started it."

Ben Krane owned a lot of property. Too much, in the opinion of a lot of people. I looked at Corrie. "Where was the fire?"

He thought, then waved a hand in a gesture that took in most of the island. "Over there in what they call Arbutus Park. Or so they tell me. I never been there, myself."

Zee smiled at him. "You want a ride to the church tonight?"

"No, thank you. Some ladies from the guild are going to pick me up and bring me back."

"Fine. I hope we can get in. I think they may have a lot bigger congregation tonight than usual."

"I'll save you a couple of seats in the front row."

"Super," said Zee, and we drove away.

As we approached Arbutus Park, I could smell the sour stench of smoke. It got stronger as we turned up the bumpy sand road that led away from the highway and into the woods.

"I hope the girl is okay," said Zee. "Fire scares me more than most things. Do you know where you're going?"

"There's an old farmhouse up here a ways that always looked to me like a typical Ben Krane place."

"You mean it looks like a dump and every summer it's filled with college kids."

"That's what I mean."

"I guess you're right. There's a fire truck."

We stopped on the road across from the blackened ruins of the house. There wasn't much left. A few wisps of smoke still drifted into the air, watched by some of Edgartown's volunteer firemen. One of them was Frank Costa. He came over.

"Went up like a torch," he said. "Good thing nobody was at home."

"What started it?" asked Zee.

"Too soon to say. Could be anything. Cigarette, bad wiring, you name it."

"Arson?"

The possibility didn't seem to surprise Frank. "Could be, I guess. No hydrants anywhere close, pretty isolated spot, so nobody much would be around after the kids went off to that party. We had a bunch of arsons in places like this a few years back. You remember them?"

"I remember."

He yawned. "I been here all day. I'm ready to hit the sack." He turned and looked down the road, and when he did I could hear the sound of a car. "Well, well," said Frank. "Here comes the owner, I do believe."

I looked in the rearview mirror and saw a new Land Rover coming up the road. It parked behind us and Ben Krane got out and looked angrily at the ruin.

He was a tall, handsome man with a face like a hawk's. He was twice divorced, but, according to gossip, women who weren't married to him found him fascinating. He always seemed to have an attractive one around, anyway, though rarely the same one for too long. He and I bumped into each other now and then, and I had no fault to find with him other than his profession as slumlord.

Zee's views were stronger. She considered him a creep.

"Not much left standing, Ben," said Frank.

"When's the fire marshal going to get here?" snapped Ben.

"Not much he can do till things cool down and he can get in there," said Frank.

"The sooner the better. One of those damned kids probably left a cigarette someplace. I ought to make them take out insurance!"

"Trust Ben to come up with another way to squeeze money out of somebody," hissed Zee. "Come to think of it, I'm surprised he doesn't already do that. He could do it through his own company and make money coming and going."

"Down, Fang. Maybe he's just a shocked landlord, distraught with grief."

"Ben Krane has never been distraught about anything in his life. You have to have feelings to be distraught!"

Ben glanced our way, then came over to the car and leaned down. "Hello, J.W., what brings you out this way? Hello, Zee. Haven't seen you for a while."

"Hello, Ben," said Zee. "No, it's been a while. Did I hear you say you burned this place down for the insurance?"

He managed to place a thin smile on his falcon face. "Same old Zee, always quick with the quip. These your kids? Pair of cuties. Little girl looks just like you, Zee. She's going to grow up to be a beauty, J.W. You'll be fighting off the boys in a few years." He straightened and looked at his Rolex. "Well, I'm going to circumnavigate what's left of this place, then I have to get back to work."

He walked toward the smoking remains of the house.

"I wouldn't be surprised if he actually did torch it," said Zee. "It's probably insured for more than it's worth and he's already collected his summer rent. He gets it up front and the kids will have to sue him to get it back."

"I imagine those thoughts will cross the fire marshal's mind," I said, putting the old Toyota in gear. Fires are like killings. They may be accidental or they may be on purpose, but if they're on purpose, the first suspects are people close to the casualty. Of course, strangers commit crimes, too, but not as often as you might think. We usually get robbed or killed by our friends and families, and a lot of people burn down their own buildings.

We drove home to get ready for Corrie's concert in Oak Bluffs. We wanted to look respectable so Corrie wouldn't be embarrassed to be seen with us.

Zee sniffed at her sleeve and wrinkled her nose. "We all smell like smoke," she said. "These clothes will have to be washed."

I remembered a fire that had made me sick the first year I was a cop in Boston. A guy had been smoking in bed and had burned himself up. The whole apartment had smelled like cooked hot dogs.

Day-trippers to the Vineyard usually land in Oak Bluffs, so the docks and Circuit Avenue, its main street, are lined with snack-food joints and gift shops offering Taiwan-made Martha's Vineyard mementos to visitors who have circumnavigated the island in tour buses and are now heading back to the mainland prepared to give authoritative reports about the place.

Seeing them boarding the boat for their return trip to the mainland, I am reminded of the time when I was lying on the beach in the summer sun, and overheard two college-age girls talking about their plans for the next year. One of them said she was going to Europe. The other replied, "Oh, I've seen that place. I was there on spring break."

Never having been to Europe, I was aware that I was in no position to criticize the girl who had apparently seen it all in a week. Similarly, since I've never taken the tour bus around the Vineyard, I try to withhold judgment of the knowledge of island day-trippers, too.

Oak Bluffs is also one of the two towns on the Vineyard that allow alcohol to be sold and served, and is the site of a couple of notorious bars, including the Fireside, where I have been known to lift a glass or two. All in all, OB is the funkiest town on the island, and OB people wouldn't live anywhere else.

The church where Corrie was performing was already overflowing when Zee and I got there, but the big guy at the door was expecting us and showed us to our reserved seats in the front row, leading us past slightly irked people who had gotten there before us but were obliged to stand if they were going to hear Corrie.

It was a mostly dark-complected crowd, but there were paler people, too. I recognized some of the folks seated in the pews: John and Mattie Skye; Stanley Crandel, the latest in a long line of Crandels who owned the big Crandel house on East Chop, and who liked to claim John Saunders, the slave turned Methodist preacher, as an ancestor; his wife, Betsy, who waved; their actress niece, Julie Crandel, who was visiting from Hollywood and also waved; and, seated across the hall away from the more respectable Crandels, the small, ageless figures of Cousin Henry Bayles and his wife. Cousin Henry, who reputedly had once run the black mobs in Philadelphia, but was now quietly retired in a cottage down by Lagoon Pond, did not wave.

Since it was a house of God, the minister led a rousing prayer of thanks for grace and music, and turned the evening over to Corrie, who led off with a number I remembered hearing him sing with my father long long ago.

The blues tell of hard times and down times, of lonesome times, of sin and sorrow, of prisons with and without bars; but they also speak of endurance, of outlasting adversity, of good times with good women and good liquor.

Corrie sang mourning songs of ropes, chain gangs, and cotton fields, but mixed them with soft songs of rocking chairs on Southern summer porches, of bedrooms and barrooms that were warm and friendly, at least for a time. Sometimes we clapped hands as he sang, sometimes we sat and just listened to that voice of his, which he never raised, but that carried to the farthest corners of the hall. It delivered despair and hope without sentimentality or self-pity, and when Corrie put aside his guitar for the last time, the audience was left with emotions of both joy and sorrow, right where the blues usually leave you. As Corrie shook hands with the Crandels and others who surrounded him, the rest of us slowly exited into the night, feeling sad and good and somehow wiser than we had just a couple of hours earlier.

As we went out the door, we looked back and I saw Corrie embrace Cousin Henry Bayles and kiss Henry's wife.

"Well," said Zee, holding my hand as we walked to the truck. "That was mighty fine. I thought I heard some Brownie McGhee and maybe some Gary Davis in there, along with the other stuff."

"Could be. Reverend Gary worked with a lot of guys. I wouldn't be surprised if Corrie was one of them."

"I see that Corrie and Cousin Henry are close."

"Maybe Corrie spent some time in Philly when Cousin Henry was down there. As I understand it, Cousin Henry owned some clubs or at least took some money out of them before he left town for good. Maybe Corrie worked in some of them. He's mixed with some tough birds in some tough places, from what he says."

"I'm glad to learn that Cousin Henry likes the blues. It makes him seem more human."

My mouth said, "He's as human as most of us, I think."

But in my mind I wasn't so sure. The cop's jungle telegraph, to which I had been hooked while on the Boston PD, had it that Cousin Henry had done some very, very bad things to people while in Philadelphia. Admittedly, the victims were pretty bad themselves, for the most part, and would have done to Henry what he had done to them, had they gotten the chance. Still, if the rumors were even somewhat true, at least part of Cousin Henry was arguably more beast than human.

But then there are monsters inside of most of us, just waiting to get out.

We drove home and relieved the twin of her baby-sitting duties.

"How was the concert? Were Mom and Daddy there?"

"Great and yes. A good time was had by all."

"How long is Mr. Appleyard going to be on the island? I hear that there's going to be a big party at a house tomorrow night, and that everybody's going to take something for the kids who got burned out, and that they wanted Mr. Appleyard to sing a couple of songs for the cause, but he's leaving the island before the party, so he can't do it."

"How did you hear about all that?"

Only the faintest of blushes touched the twin's cheeks. "I used your phone a little. I hope you don't mind."

We didn't mind, so the twin accepted her money, assured us that our offspring had been angels, got into her mother's car, and left.

"It would be encouraging to think that these summer kids would actually want to hear the blues," said Zee. "Maybe I've misjudged them. Too bad Corrie can't be there."

"I'd like to think some of them have good taste in music," I said, "but I don't have any reason to."

"We're becoming old fuddy-duddies, just like my parents," sighed Zee. "They didn't like the music I liked, and now I don't like the music the next generation likes."

As one who was born disliking most of whatever music was currently popular—preferring country-and-western and classical, and having a selective taste for traditional English, Scottish, Irish, and Russian ballads, some jazz and some blues—I did not instantly admit to fuddy-duddyism.

"Maybe it's the sweaty-bed blues they like," I said, easing up to her and starting to unbutton her shirt.

Her blue-black hair smelled sweet and musky, and her dark eyes were deep as the sea. "Maybe that's it," she said, unbuttoning my shirt in return. "Makes sense to me."

I slid her shirt off her shoulders and kissed her right there on that spot at the base of her throat. She put her arms around my neck. I picked her up and carried her into the bedroom.

Marriage is good for you.

The next day, Joshua and I worked on the addition, with Diana supervising from her corral. It was pretty clear that I'd probably get more done without assistance, but so what? I wanted my kids to know how to swing hammers, fish, and do the other stuff that I did. As we worked, the *pop-pop-pop* of gunfire came through the trees from the Rod and Gun Club. One of the poppers was Zee, using her custom .45.

Zee was practicing at the club range with Manny Fonseca, who was her tutor in the competitive pistol-shooting game they played. In spite of her belief that the world would be a better place without firearms, Zee was a whiz with a pistol and had begun to make a name for herself shooting competitively.

She also had a lot of fun, which was something she had expected even less than her discovery that she was what Manny called a natural with a handgun. Her moral convictions about weapons were thus at odds with her talent and the pleasure shooting gave her, but the conflict didn't prevent her from being a better pistol shot than I had ever been, even when I'd packed iron professionally, first as a soldier and then as a cop. Like Scarlett O'Hara, I could shoot pretty well as long as I didn't have to shoot too far. Zee was a veritable Joanna Wayne.

In time, she and I would teach our children about pistols, rifles, and shotguns, for ignorance of weapons is, like ignorance of most things, more dangerous than knowledge. But that would come later, when they were older and bigger. For now, as the sounds of Manny's and Zee's practice rounds came snapping at us through the trees, Joshua and Diana were apprentice carpenters.

That afternoon, after cleaning her pistol and making note of an upcoming competition over in America, Zee went off to work on the four-to-midnight shift.

No doubt there would be plenty of work waiting for her. The emergency ward at the hospital in OB took in a pretty steady stream of customers during the summer, including moped casualties; sufferers of sprains, contusions, broken bones, heart problems, alcohol and drug overdoses; and other routine patients. I don't think I could ever do the work of medics without becoming hard as granite, but Zee, like most nurses and doctors I've met, somehow managed to stay quite human. It's almost enough to make you believe that there is a God.

Not long after she left, Corrie Appleyard, looking none too well, came putt-putting down the driveway on the same moped he'd been working on earlier.

"Easy rider," he said with a forced smile. "Just came by to say good-bye, and thanks. I'm catching the seven-thirty boat back to the mainland." He put out his long brown hand and shook mine.

"Zee's gone to work," I said. "She'll be sorry to have missed you. We'll have a room ready for you in the fall, so come back anytime."

"Sorry to have missed your wife," said Corrie, "but I'll take you up on that offer to visit." He lifted a hand. "It's been nice meeting your family. See you next time."

He drove back up the driveway and out of sight.

That night, sometime after Zee came home, climbed into bed beside me, and we both snuggled to sleep, I was awakened by the fire whistle in Edgartown calling to the volunteers. Then I heard sirens and more sirens, and I was disturbed by the direction they seemed to be headed. I listened, then eased out of bed and went into the living room and turned on the scanner. Voices and static crackled from the speaker. I heard the name of the street where Corrie had been staying, and had an almost irresistible urge to go there. But I knew that the last thing the firemen needed was another citizen getting in their way, so I remained where I was.

In time I heard someone say that the place seemed to be empty, and I felt a surge of relief. Apparently, everybody had gone to a party at another house, said the voice.

That would be the party the twin had mentioned, where the college kids would combine fun with charity as they tried to help those who'd gotten burned out earlier, and where Corrie had been asked to do some singing for the good cause.

Another bad fire, but at least no one had gotten hurt, in spite of the arsonist who I now believed was pretty clearly at work. The fire marshal could handle it. I turned off the scanner and went back to bed.

It wasn't until the next morning, as I made breakfast and listened to the radio news, that I learned I was wrong about no one being hurt. A body, as yet unidentified, had been found in the ruined remains of the house.

— 10 —

Is there a worse death than death by fire? According to what I'd read, most victims in fires died not from flames but of suffocation, often while they slept, so maybe it was quicker and less painful than other deaths. Maybe the real horror of fire was experienced by those who survived the flames. I, at least, could imagine no more dismaying fate. My acrophobia and claustrophobia shrank to nothing by comparison. Better by far to fall or even smother to death than to be maimed by fire. My father's life as a fireman in Somerville had never inspired me to follow in his professional footsteps; another career course, that of a policeman, had seemed a much safer one to me.

Of course, policemen run risks, too, and my five years on the Boston PD had ended abruptly in the shooting that had left me with a bullet that still snuggled against my spine. But somehow even now, years later, being shot didn't seem nearly as frightening as being burned to death.

Zee and I listened to the radio for details but got few: a fire, the body of a person whose identity was being withheld until relatives could be informed, the building a total loss.

I poured Zee's coffee and she looked up at me and said, "You say the sirens sounded like they were headed toward the house where Corrie was staying."

I thought that's what the scanner had said. "I can't be sure," I said. The morning wind was from the southwest and I wondered if I was imagining the smell of smoke floating down our long driveway.

"I think we should go and see," said Zee. "If that boy Adam got burned out, we can put him up for a few days until he gets his feet back on the ground."

"Maybe it wasn't even his house," I said. "There are a lot of houses in that area."

"We should go see," said Zee. "Maybe we can help." She put her cup aside and got to her feet.

"Maybe one of us should stay here with the kids."

"They'll be fine. They'll stay in the car."

She rose and we cleared the table and stacked the morning dishes in the sink. We put Joshua and Diana in the old Land Cruiser and drove to the house where Corrie had been staying.

It was a blackened ruin smoldering amid scorched trees and piles of water-soaked rubble. Firemen played hoses on the fallen walls while smoke drifted away downwind. There were several disheveled young people sitting or standing, looking at the remains of what had once been their summerhouse. I recognized a few faces I'd seen when I'd brought Corrie home. One of them was the boy who'd told us about Adam being missing. I also saw Ben Krane circling the ruin, his face dark and angry.

I parked and went over to the boy. "Have you seen Adam Washington?"

He gave me a vague look. "Adam? Yeah. He's around here somewhere. Maybe he went to work, come to think of it. I'm not sure."

"How could he go to work when all his clothes are cinders?"

An ironic smile flitted over his face. "Adam works on a garbage truck. He doesn't need clean clothes. Most of the rest of us do."

I felt a small flicker of approval for Adam Washington, a college kid who was willing to work on a garbage truck.

We looked at the smoking house for a moment, then I said, "Were you here when they found the body in there?"

He shrugged. "I guess so. We were all here watching our stuff go up in flames after the firemen came. Nobody told us when they found the body, but we saw them bring something out on a stretcher and put it in the ambulance. I guess that was it."

"Did you see who it was?"

"Jesus, no! It was in a bag."

From some recess of my mind a closed door opened and I saw once again the boxer pose of that long-ago charred victim who had burned himself to death in his own bed. I again smelled boiled hot dogs and nearly retched. Was it a real smell from this site or the memory of that one I'd smelled in Boston long ago?

Frank Costa, looking tired as death, was drinking a cup of coffee by a fire truck. I went over.

"I've had enough fires for a while," he said. "They better catch this torcher quick."

"You should go home and let some of the other guys manage this."

He shrugged. "Everybody's in the same boat."

"So you think it was arson."

"Two fires in two of Ben Krane's houses in the same week? What do you think?"

"I think you're probably right."

"I ain't a fire marshal or an arson investigator," said Frank. "I'm only a gardener who volunteers for this work, so I could be wrong."

"So could I, but I don't think so. Did you see the body they found?"

"Hell, I was the one who saw it first. First one I ever seen. Had them bent arms you read about. Like a boxer, you know. Fire contracts the muscles or something like that; I forget." He drank his coffee, his sooty face lined with fatigue and his red eyes weary and vague.

"Was it a man or a woman?"

"Hell, don't ask me. I couldn't tell by looking at it."

"Big or small? Tall or short?"

"I don't know. I didn't look too close."

"I guess I wouldn't either."

Frank yawned. "I need about twenty-four hours of sleep, J.W., or I ain't gonna be worth a damn when I go back to work. Maybe I'm getting too old for this firefighting stuff."

"Nah," I said, "you're good for another twenty years."

Frank had been with Edgartown's volunteer fire department as long as I could remember. When I'd been just a kid, he'd been a fireman, and he, a small-town, amateur fireman, and my dad, a big-city professional fireman, had enjoyed a summer friendship whenever my father and my sister and I had come to the island for a holiday. Right now, he was about as old as my father had been when that warehouse wall had fallen on him.

"There you are," said a voice behind me. "I've been looking for you."

I turned and saw Ben Krane. His falcon face was gray with soot and his suit trousers and shoes were black from the ashes he'd been walking through as he'd circled and studied the ruins of his house. His dark eyes were narrow and hot. Beyond him, I could see Zee looking at us from the Land Cruiser.

I said, "If this keeps up, you won't have any houses left, Ben."

"You're damned right about that! This is the third building I've lost since spring. Somebody is trying to burn me out of business!" He glared at Frank. "And nobody is doing anything about it! Not a damned thing. They haven't got a clue about who's doing it or why!"

Frank was tired and irritable enough to tell the truth. "A lot of people wish you were out of business, Krane. You own half the slums on Martha's Vineyard!" He put down his coffee cup and straightened. He was twenty years older than Krane, five inches shorter, and about forty pounds lighter. Krane, eyes ablaze, stepped toward him. I slipped between them.

"What can I do for you, Ben?"

His eyes were level with mine, and he almost put a hand on me to push me aside. But then he caught himself and stepped back.

"I want you to find out who's doing this. The fire people and the cops are doing nothing! If I leave it to them, I may as well burn my places down myself!"

"Some people think you're doing that already," said Frank, trying to get around my outstretched arm.

"Finish your coffee, Frank," I said. "Let's step away from here, Ben. Come on."

Ben hesitated, glaring at Frank, who, I imagined, was glaring back, then allowed me to walk him away from the fire truck.

"I know what people think of me," he said, when we stopped a distance away, "and I don't give a damn. I pay my taxes and I give good service to the people who hire me. I play it straight as a realtor and as a lawyer and as a landlord. I don't care whether people like me or not. All I want is to be treated the same way as everybody else!" He glanced at Frank with angry eyes.

The speech sounded rehearsed to me, but maybe it wasn't. I thought that at least part of it was true: Ben really didn't give a damn about what people thought of him.

I hadn't eased him away from Frank so we could discuss his proposal to hire me, because I thought that idea was nonsense; I'd done it to get him and Frank apart.

"I know you must be frustrated," I said, "but I don't think I'm the guy you should be hiring. I don't know a thing about arson or arsonists, and the cops and the arson investigators are professionals; you should leave it up to them to find this guy, whoever he is."

"I lost an office last year and three houses this year, and they haven't found shit! I need somebody working for *me*!"

"If you think you have to hire somebody, you should hire a professional investigator. Try Thornberry Security up in Boston. They're about as good as you can get."

Krane shook his head. "What does a Boston outfit know about Martha's Vineyard? No, I want somebody who knows his way around."

"All right," I said. "I'll work on it for a week. After that, you can find somebody else." I named an outrageous fee, but instead of telling me to forget the whole thing, he surprised me by nodding.

"Fine," he said, and I had a job I didn't want.

11

Krane put out his big hand and I automatically took it.

"Thanks," he said. "I'll put a check in the mail for the week's work."

Beyond him, I saw Zee frown at the handshake.

"Before you mail that check, there are some things you should consider," I said. "You may find out something you don't want to know, or I may find out something you don't want other people to know." Not long before, I'd said much the same thing to Susanna Quick. In reply, he said much the same thing that she had, but with a different tone.

His eyes narrowed. "You'll be working for me. You'll report to me, not to anyone else."

"If I find out who did this, I don't plan on keeping it a secret. The cops and the fire marshal will need to know."

He waved an impatient hand. "Fine. Tell them that. But don't tell them anything they don't need to know."

I pushed further. "I may find out something you don't want *me* to know."

"I expect you to be discreet."

"Everybody has secrets," I said. "You're no different. I may have to pry around your life more than you want."

He frowned. "Leave me and my life out of this. Just find the guy who's burning down my houses."

"Whoever you hire will be digging into your life. In fact, the cops and fire marshal probably already are."

His brows lowered. "What? Why?"

"You're a lawyer, you should know. When there's a crime, there are always two stories involved: the crimi-

nal's story and the victim's story. When the two stories
come together, the crime takes place. To find the connec-
tion, everybody working the case may want to know more
about you than you want them to. The cops are probably
already looking for the link, and I will be, too."

His face was hard. "I don't like this."

He irked me. "We can call this deal off right now. But if
you want me to work for you, I'll need to know about the
things you do that might have pissed somebody off
enough to start burning down your houses. The guy may
just think of himself as a humanitarian doing his bit to
make the Vineyard a better place to live, but I doubt it. I
think it's probably personal. Unless you're burning the
places down yourself for the insurance money. That's
another possibility."

"That's slander!"

I'd had enough of him. "It's a thought that's probably
crossed more minds than mine. It looks to me like we
can't do business. Find yourself another investigator." I
walked away.

"Wait."

I turned back and saw him will his face free of rage.

"Wait," he said again through gritted teeth. "You're
wrong, but you're right. I didn't torch these places, but I
know that some people probably think I did. Maybe if I
were my insurer or somebody in the fire marshal's office,
I'd suspect me of doing just that. But I didn't do it. And I
want to find out who did. I'll work with you any way you
want."

I doubted that, but it was a start. "All right. Tell the people in your office to talk to me when I come by."

"What have they got to do with anything?" He was
instantly on guard again. Like a lot of bosses, I suspected,
he liked to keep his workers in the dark about some things.

"They may know something useful to me."

"Like what?"

"How should I know? Maybe I'll find out when I talk

with them." I studied him. "Are we going to tangle like this over everybody I want to talk to and everything I want to know?"

He took a deep breath. "No."

"Good."

He wasn't ready to drop control, though. "I'll fire you if you go too far."

I nodded. "And I'll quit if you don't let me do my job."

A small, perhaps bitter smile sliced across his face. "The check for a week's work will be in the mail."

"I'll keep you informed about what I find out. But don't get your hopes up. I'm no arson investigator. I still think you should leave this to the pros." I turned and walked back to the Land Cruiser.

"Just find out who did this and stop him," he said from behind me.

"What was that all about?" asked Zee as I reached the truck.

I told her, and watched a scowl mar her beautiful face. "I don't like you working for that man."

"We can use the money," I said. "Besides, I don't like the idea of an arsonist running around town. He might decide to burn us down next."

"Ben Krane is a scumbag."

I didn't think she was going to change her mind, and I wasn't going to change mine, so I changed the subject instead. "Have you seen Adam Washington?"

"No." Her voice was sharp.

"Ma, what's a scumbag?" asked Joshua from the backseat.

"I think I'll go look for Adam while you educate our son," I said. I smiled down upon the inquisitive child's angry mother and walked away.

I found a college boy back among the trees, sitting beside the moped that Corrie Appleyard had ridden into our yard. He had the look of a battle-weary soldier: face lined and dirty, shoulders sagging. He looked up at me with vacant, guilty eyes.

"Have you seen Adam Washington?" I asked.

He shook his head. He looked as though he might cry but had no tears within him. "No."

"Have you seen Millicent Dowling?"

The question seemed to make no sense to him. Finally, he gave a slight shrug. "She's gone away someplace."

"Where?"

He stared at me, then said, "I don't know."

"Where were you when this started?"

He considered the question as though it was of little interest, then waved a languid hand. "I was over at the party with everybody else. We were all over there. And while we were gone, this happened. Jesus, all they have in this town is fires. Every fucking house on the island is burning down."

"Was Adam at the party?"

He nodded. "He was there for a while at least. I was drinking beer and not paying much attention." He nodded toward the ruin. "I wonder if that was him they found in there. I keep thinking that if I'd stayed at home last night, I could have kept this from happening. I feel like it's my fault." He sounded like a penitent in a confessional admitting to some sin.

But I was no priest and had no spiritual solace for him. "It probably wasn't Adam in there" was all I could offer.

"I think it was him," he said. "It's all my fault."

I didn't think so, but the boy did. As somebody said, man is the only animal that blushes or needs to. In this case, the boy was deep in guilt over something that he had nothing to do with. We are strange creatures.

"You have a place to stay?" I asked.

"No, but I'll find some place or other." He waved at the smoking walls. "All my stuff was in there, but it wasn't much. I can get more."

I looked past him at the moped and saw what looked like the side of a guitar case that was leaning against the back of the same tree. I stepped around the tree and opened the case. Corrie's old Martin was in there, and I knew when I saw it that Corrie was dead, because he'd never have left the guitar out there if he were alive.

Feeling cold and clinical, I took out the guitar and looked through the case. I found some picks and a couple of capos and some scribbled notes of what looked like songs in the making. Nothing else.

I put the guitar back into the case and carried it back to the boy.

"This is Corrie Appleyard's guitar," I said. "It'll go to his family. You know where I can get in touch with them?"

He looked at me with his dull, guilt-stricken eyes. "No. How should I know that? I don't know anything about his family."

"Adam Washington is the grandson of a friend of his." I looked into my brain for the name and came out with it. "Ernie Washington. Did Adam ever mention Ernie Washington or Corrie's family?"

"I don't remember ever hearing anything about those people."

There wasn't anything more that either of us could give to the other. I looked at the ruin.

"You didn't do this," I said. "It just happened. It wasn't your fault."

"No," he insisted, "it was my fault. If it hadn't been for me, it wouldn't have happened."

Some people refuse to be comforted. The boy seemed to be the type, and since I only have limited patience with people who like to feel guilty, I ended the conversation and went back to the Land Cruiser.

Zee was stiff-faced as I put the guitar case in the back and climbed behind the wheel. I ignored her expression and told her where I'd found the case and what little the boy had told me.

She frowned. "What was Corrie's guitar doing out there?" Then, "Oh my gosh!"

"Yeah," I said. "Corrie wouldn't have left the island without his guitar."

She looked at me with her great, dark eyes. "He wouldn't, would he?"

"I don't think so," I said. "I don't know, but I don't think so."

In her eyes I saw pity and sorrow and felt like I was seeing a reflection of my own. The eyes are the windows of the soul, they say. I put my hand on her thigh and she put her hand over mine.

12

At home we said nothing more about me working for Ben Krane. For Zee and me, hot-and-heavy disagreements were not a regular thing, and we were therefore not well practiced in dealing with such events. However, we each knew the other's stubbornness and anger span (in my case, two days, max, before I tended to forget why I'd been mad), and thus had mutually adopted a wait-it-out policy of conflict resolution. Screamers, some say, get arguments out of their systems fairly quickly, but we who are inclined toward sullenness and silence take longer.

The best thing was to stay off each other's toes while feelings were young and tender, so I left Zee at the house with her still-inquisitive son ("Are there lots of scumbags, Ma?") and took Diana the Huntress with me as I drove downtown.

Edgartown in June was not nearly so crowded as it would become in July and August, but already the streets were full of pale-skinned tourists peeking into shop windows; nibbling on goodies from the delis, ice cream parlors, and candy stores; and wandering blithely in front of cars. Vineyard visitors apparently think that the island is a make-believe place, like Disneyland, so they feel free to casually walk in the middle of the streets since the automobiles are only props. Fortunately, most local drivers are used to this and are very careful not to run over anyone.

Helping them out are the Edgartown police, who do their best to keep things moving but safe for one and all. I found the chief down by the town hall, telling yet another bicyclist that Main Street was forbidden territory for two-wheelers. The cyclist went away, pushing her bike.

"You know you're wasting your time, don't you?" I said, coming up as the cyclist was leaving. "Bicycle riders are illiterate. They can't read signs. Especially signs that say 'No bicycles.'"

"If you mean I'm shoveling shit against the tide, you're right," he said. "But that's a policeman's lot. We do it for a living. We try to keep people from breaking the law, but they break it anyway. And if we catch them, the bondsmen bail them out, the lawyers get them off, and the judges let them go."

He didn't sound too sour, however; he was just realistic. Actually, cops spend most of their time on jobs having little to do with crime as such. Besides directing traffic and patrolling the roads, they break up domestic arguments before they get violent, help fallen elderly to get back in bed, and PC drunks for the night and let them go again the next morning. They help round up farm animals that are loose on the roads, and they tote people to the emergency room of the hospital. Most of the violence they encounter is in the form of accidents: drunks and teens driving their cars into trees at high rates of speed, moped riders spilling themselves onto the pavement, or people chopping off their toes while mowing the lawn.

From time to time, of course, they meet with criminal violence. The wife beater, the pedophile, the knifer, the robber, the man with a gun.

The arsonist.

I'd left the Boston PD to get away from all that, but of course there is no away and no man is an island even on an island, so here I was, nosing around in the very business I'd once forsworn.

The chief looked at Diana, who was riding on my back in her canvas kid-holder. He put out a hand to her. "Hello."

From the corner of my eye, I saw her little hand meet his. "How do you do?" said her small voice.

"You look like your mother," said the chief. Then he looked at me. "Fortunately."

The chief had grandchildren older than Diana.

"She has her mother's looks, but my brains and ready wit," I said.

"I'm sorry to hear that, kid," said the chief, looking back at her. "Maybe things will work out for you anyway."

"We're going to get ice cream," said Diana.

"In a little while," I said. "First I have to talk to the chief, here."

"I knew the day was going too well," said the chief. "What do you want?"

I told him about the job I'd just taken with Ben Krane. He didn't change expression, but something altered in his eyes.

"I guess Ben doesn't trust the fire marshal," he said.

"He didn't seem to when I talked to him. He thinks I have local knowledge that will make the difference."

"I didn't know you were an arson investigator, J.W. I thought you were just a fisherman living up there in the woods."

"I was at a couple of fire scenes when I worked in Boston," I said, "but all I did was glance in the rooms, then stand outside and look official while the arson squad did the real work."

"But Ben Krane wants you to work for him anyway. Doesn't make much sense to me. I always thought Ben was a bright guy. Maybe I was wrong."

"Maybe you can help me be as smart as Ben wants me to be. What can you tell me about arson investigations?"

"What do you want to know?"

"Well, for a start you can tell me who does the investigating."

"Not us local hicks, for sure. We're not smart enough to do complicated stuff like handle fires that aren't your ordinary accidental kind. No, it's the state boys who handle the arson cases. The fire marshals are part of the state police. Whenever there's a suspicious fire or a death, they come in to investigate."

"Ah. Just like with homicides or suspicious deaths of any kind. You local guys step aside and the state cops take over."

"You got it, Sherlock," said the chief. "Us country bumpkins are good enough for the stupid stuff, but we're too dim for the work that takes brains."

The chief made this familiar comment without any particular tone of annoyance in his voice, almost as though he were talking about the weather.

And why should he do otherwise? Conflict between law enforcement agencies is pretty commonplace, after all. The state cops are uncooperative with the local cops; both the state and local cops resent the federal cops; the federal cops are uncooperative with everybody, including the international cops; and so forth. The consequences of these rivalries are always bad for law enforcement, but the conflicts continue anyway, to the frustration of all involved, especially those civilians and police officers who are more interested in crime solving than in power, prestige, and point scoring. It has been argued by some of them that warring police agencies are the perps' best friends. Could be.

"Who decides that the fire marshals should be called in?" I asked.

"The fire chief. The state guys don't consider him up to making an arson investigation, but they figure he's at least sharp enough to suspect that it may have happened. Of course, if somebody dies in the fire, the marshals get an automatic call."

"So the marshal is here already, because of the body?"

He nodded. "But it's not *marshal* in this case. It's *marshals*. Two of them. Don't ask me why. They should be up at the house any time now."

I thought about that and said, "Were they here after the other house burned a couple of nights ago?"

He looked at me. "Not that I know of. When that house burned, everybody thought it was an accident. I imagine there are some doubts about that theory now, though, so I expect Mr. and Mrs. Dings may take a good look at that place, too."

"Mr. and Mrs. Dings? Married arson investigators?"

"Jack and Sandy. Apparently they're a team. Where he goes, she goes; where she goes, he goes. Maybe I should give my wife a badge."

"I don't think she'd take it. She sees enough of you already. Where are they staying while they're down here?"

"None of your business. You take my advice, you'll stay out of the Dingses' hair. They take their work seriously and they do not suffer fools gladly."

Another illiterate cyclist came down the street, and the chief stepped out and held up his hand. The cyclist, looking surprised, stopped.

"You can't ride bikes on this street," said the chief in a gentle voice.

"Oh."

"There's a sign right up there that tells you that. You have to turn left onto Church Street."

"Oh." The cyclist looked vaguely back up the street.

"There are bike racks at the end of Church Street on Pease's Point Way. Or you can walk your bike on down Main." The chief smiled a warm, small-town smile.

"Oh. Okay. Sorry."

"Tell your friends about the sign and have a good day."

"Thanks."

The chief stepped back and the cyclist, walking his bike, went down the street.

"How come you never smile at me like that?" I asked. "I never see that nice palsy-walsy face looking at me."

"I'll make you a deal," said the chief. "You move off island and only come back for a week each year and I'll pretend to be friendly to you, too. It'd be worth a smile to be rid of you most of the year."

"What a thing to say to a man with his little baby daughter listening to every word."

The chief gave Diana the smile he wouldn't give to me. "Now don't you worry, sweetie, you can stay and your mom and your brother can stay; it's just your old man that's got to go."

A small hand tugged at my ear. "Pa, I want some ice cream."

"Diana the Huntress is always seeking food," I explained. "I'll see you later."

"I'm sure." I was about four steps down the street when he added, "I think the Dingses are staying up at the Wesley, in OB."

I looked back, but he was already walking up the sidewalk.

The chief was crusty but digestible. Diana and I went into the first ice cream shop we came to and laid down our money. Black raspberry for me, and chocolate chip for the kid. Because I didn't want chocolate hair, we ate in the shop, which, fortunately, had a good stock of paper napkins, since Diana was not too fastidious about her food and tended to chocolatize her face pretty well whenever encountering her favorite dessert.

When we were through and I had her scrubbed as clean as I was going to get her, I returned her to her backpack and headed for my next stop: Ben Krane's office. It was as good a time as any to beard the lion in his den.

Krane Associates was housed in a white-fronted building just off Main Street. I didn't know who the associates might be, but the business offered expertise in the law, real estate, estate planning, and other matters. Ben personally had his hand in all of these enterprises, and for all I knew, he might have had a whole team of experts working for him. When I went into the office, however, I was met by a single receptionist. According to the name card in front of her computer, she was Judith Gomes.

Judith gave me a pleasant, professional smile.

"Hi. May I help you? My, what a darling little girl!"

"My daughter, Diana. Yes, she is a cutie, if I do say so myself."

"I'm sure you're very proud of her! Now, how may I help you?"

I sat down. "My name is Jackson. I work for your boss. I want to talk with you about him and his work."

Her smile disappeared faster than your lap when you stand.

13

Judith Gomes was instantly careful, almost hostile. "I'm afraid I can't help you, Mr. . . . ."

"Jackson. My friends call me J.W."

"I'm afraid I can't help you, Mr. Jackson. I have nothing to say about Mr. Krane."

I studied her face. Judith looked a little fragile behind her apparent anger. "Did he tell you to say that, or are you just being a loyal employee? If he told you to say it, you tell him that I'm no longer working for him. If he didn't, then it's you who may not be working for him."

But Judith turned out to have more spunk than I had guessed. "I haven't spoken with Mr. Krane, and I have no intention of speaking to you either. Please leave this office immediately."

Is there anyone more valuable to a boss than a loyal secretary who will fend off the dogs and keep the family secrets?

I felt a little smile run across my face. "I think you should ask Ben for a raise," I said. "Meanwhile, if you can get in touch with him, I suggest that you do that right now. He asked me to work for him this morning and gave me carte blanche to do things my own way, including talking to you and anybody else who works for him. You, naturally, don't believe that, so why don't you pick up that phone and get the word from the horse's mouth."

Her jaw was firm. "Mr. Krane is not in his office. I don't know where he is. I'll speak to him when he comes in."

Feisty Judith. "He's probably got a beeper on his belt

like all the other businesspeople in the world," I said. "Give him a buzz."

She was stubborn. "I don't think so, Mr. Jackson!"

I bounced Diana on my knee. She was cute. Playing with her and her brother was a more appealing prospect than tracking down an arsonist. "In that case," I said to Judith Gomes, "when you finally do talk to Ben, tell him about our conversation and inform him that I'm not working for him anymore. Tell him I'll return his check if he's already mailed it." I got out of the chair. "Good-bye. I don't think we'll be seeing each other again." I started for the door.

"Wait."

I paused and looked at her. Her brow was furrowed as she was pricked by the famous horns of a dilemma: in her case, whether to risk offending her boss by calling him, or risk offending him by not calling him. Her hand seemed to want to go to the phone on her desk, but . . .

I decided to help her out. "Look," I said, "if he hasn't told you about this deal with me, you'd be stupid to take my word for it. Be smart and call him. If he faults you for that, he's more of an idiot than I think he is."

"If you're telling the truth, I would have heard from him already." But the brow remained furrowed.

"We just made the deal. He probably didn't figure I'd be snooping around here so soon. His mistake. Give him a call."

Her fingers danced on the desk and then went to the phone. They tapped out some numbers and then put the phone down. "He'll call back," she said coldly.

Sure enough, a minute or two later the phone rang and she picked it up. She listened, then gave a brief and accurate account of our encounter in the office. She listened again, said good-bye, and put the phone down. She waved at the chair I'd just abandoned. "Please sit down, Mr. Jackson."

"My friends call me J.W." I sat down with Diana on my knee.

"I'm not sure we're friends, Mr. Jackson, but I've been instructed to answer any questions you might have."

I bounced Diana. She smiled. It was her first interrogation, but she wasn't really paying attention to it. She was concentrating on the bouncing. I looked over her head at Judith Gomes.

I asked the questions and for a while Judith Gomes answered them:

She'd been working for him for six years. Yes, he was a good boss. He paid her well and never asked her to do anything illegal or even questionable. No, he didn't have any enemies. Yes, he was an honest man. No, he never cheated anybody. Yes, he charged a lot for his summer rentals, but no one was forced to pay his prices; they could pay or rent elsewhere.

Saint Benjamin of Edgartown. I tried to tilt the halo.

"A lot of people will tell you he's a slumlord whose buildings are hovels."

She lifted her chin. "A lot of people are envious fools."

"You'll have to admit that he's not the most popular guy in town."

"I never pay attention to gossip."

"Maybe you should. Somebody seems to be burning down his houses. Who do you think that might be?"

"A madman. Somebody with a psychological problem."

"Or maybe somebody with a grudge."

"I can't imagine who that might be. Mr. Krane is an honest businessman."

The halo was secure.

I smiled down at Diana, then up at Judith Gomes. "I don't know much about arson, but I do know that the owners of junky buildings sometimes burn them down for the insurance. How much insurance did Ben have on the three houses that have been torched?"

Her eyes flamed and her voice was almost a snarl. "What an awful thing to ask! How dare you! Mr. Krane would never do anything like that! You have an evil, nasty mind!"

I couldn't argue the last, but I thought her no was louder than it needed to be. I put a little metal in my voice. "There's a fire marshal on the island right now," I said, "and he's going to be interested in the insurance on those houses, too. If he finds out that Ben is making a bundle on these fires, he's got the guns to give your boss a lot more grief than I can. I don't work for the police, but if Ben had a motive for torching his own houses, I want to know about it right now. So how much insurance did he have?"

She stared at me, tight-lipped, then went to a file cabinet and came back with some papers. I reached for them and after a brief hesitation she gave them to me. Ben had the houses insured for more than I guessed they were worth. I pushed the papers back.

"He won't lose any money because these places burned down," I said.

"That's what insurance is for, Mr. Jackson." She returned the papers to the file cabinet and came back to her desk. "Those houses are rented to college students, who treat them like pigsties. They leave cigarettes lying around and plug boom boxes and God knows what else into electrical sockets. Mr. Krane would be a fool not to carry a lot of insurance, and I assure you that he is not a fool!"

"He may be too smart for his own good," I said. "Insurance companies are quick to take a client's money, but they're pretty slow to pay it out if they think they've gotten ripped off. Has he collected anything yet?"

"He hasn't even submitted a claim on these latest fires."

"How about the one that happened last spring?"

She hesitated, then shook her head. "No, he hasn't gotten a payment yet. But he will. It was definitely arson."

"I can see why his insurance company might be a little suspicious of your boss. Especially since his OB office got torched a year ago. Ben seems to collect fires."

"I resent that! Mr. Krane is above reproach."

What a loyal lady she was. I wondered what made her

that way. Even after her boss had told her to tell me whatever I wanted to know, she was only giving me good stuff. But Ben Krane was not the holy man she was making him out to be. There are no real saints on Martha's Vineyard.

"The house that burned last March was empty, wasn't it?"

"That's right."

"What do they think caused the fire?"

"Arson. I don't remember the details. I imagine you can get that information from the Edgartown fire chief."

I gave Diana a kiss on the forehead, and changed gears.

"Ben has two ex-wives still living in town. What do you know about them? Is either of them still so mad at him that she'd torch his buildings?"

"That's ridiculous. Of course not."

"Amicable separations, eh? No hard feelings, alimony satisfactory to all involved?"

She leaned forward on her elbows. "Mr. Krane married his first wife when they were both too young. It just didn't work out. They separated without acrimony. His second wife left him for another woman. Surely you've heard that story; it's common gossip. She apparently tried to be straight but gave up and went the way nature intended her to go. Again there was no acrimony. Only embarrassment for Mr. Krane. Neither woman has ever approached him for anything or expressed any anger toward him. If they had, I'd know about it."

Indeed? "Why would you know, Miss Gomes? Does Ben share his private life with you?"

She sat back. Her face was bland, but her eyes were bright. "Mr. Krane trusts me. He feels he can confide in me, and he's right. He tells me things and knows they'll go no further."

I listened and nodded and then said, "So Ben would have told you if an ex-wife was giving him grief?"

"I'm sure of it."

"Because he knew you'd never pass the information along."

She allowed herself an ironic smile. "Except when authorized to do so. As with you, Mr. Jackson."

That meant Ben was more trusting than I am. If I have any real secrets, I keep them to myself. I've wondered if that's a healthy trait, since most people I know, women in particular, seem to like to share confidences rather than keep their thoughts and feelings private. Probably it's a condition with a name familiar to students of psychology. In any case, I tell people things only if I don't mind having the information become public knowledge.

But maybe Ben wasn't as confiding as Judith Gomes thought. Maybe there were a lot of things he didn't tell her.

"How about the other women in his life?" I said. "The ones he's not married to. Does he tell you about them?"

A faint pink tone touched her cheeks. "I never inquire about his private life."

"But he certainly has one. Even I know that. He has a different woman every month."

The pink darkened to rose. "He's a very attractive man. It's only to be expected that he'd be popular with women."

I felt a touch of meanness. "He never confides in you about them?"

The rose turned almost red. "He sometimes describes an evening. A dinner, a film they saw."

"No lurid details."

"Of course not!"

Why so great a no?

"He's had a lot of women in his life, but none of them stay around too long. Why is that?"

"I'm sure I couldn't say." She glanced at her watch. It was meant to look like a quick peek, but lasted long enough not to be missed. It didn't quite irk me, but it did bring a question out of my mouth.

"Did you ever date Ben?"

Judith Gomes's face paled. "My life is none of your business!"

I waved a professorial forefinger. "Ah, ah! Ben has no secrets from me, remember."

Her jaw tightened. "If Ben . . . if Mr. Krane wants to fire me for telling you nothing about my own life, so be it!"

We eyed each other over Diana's silky-haired head.

"All right," I said. "We'll get back to you later. Tell me about Ben's family. Tell me about his brother Peter."

"I'm through talking to you today!"

Were those tears of anger, or some other sort of tears?

"I'll be back," I said.

"Get out!" Then, as though she needed some sort of a weapon against me, she almost shouted, "Your house can burn too, you know!"

I stared at her, feeling a thrill of either excitement or fear, I wasn't sure which.

14

I needed to know more about arson. There were a lot of things I needed to know, in fact. Maybe too many. It was obviously time to go to that treasure trove of information, the Edgartown Public Library.

I'd been told that the Internet was currently the information source of choice among the cognoscenti, but since I was the last computerless human being on earth, the library served the purpose for me. Libraries are some of my favorite places. They are not only full of books and papers of all kinds, but they are managed by people who both know what they're doing and actually want to be of assistance to their customers, a rare social phenomenon these days.

So Diana and I walked, hand in hand, until we got to North Water Street, then zigzagged our way through sightseeing pedestrians until we reached Edgartown's small but nifty library.

"Who's this?" asked Daisy Duarte, who was behind the front desk.

"My daughter, Diana," I said. "Say how do you do, Diana."

Diana put out her little hand. "How do you do."

"How do you do, Diana," said Daisy, taking Diana's hand in hers. "I'm Daisy. You look like your mother."

"And a good thing, too," I said.

"What brings you here today, J.W.?"

"I'm looking for information on arson."

"Oh. Are you thinking of burning something down?"

"Somebody else is ahead of me," I said. "There was another fire last night."

Daisy's smile faded. "I heard. Well, you can go right over to that monitor and find what we have."

No, I couldn't. I was fine at finding things when they had the old card files, but since the library had gone to computers I was lost. I now admitted this to Daisy.

"You should try to get into the twentieth century before it ends, J.W.," said Daisy. "Come with me, and I'll show you how to find things on our computer. It really isn't hard at all."

"Easy for you to say. I like machines that are no more complicated than a straight-bladed knife."

"Oh, don't give me that. You've kept that truck of yours going long after it should have been in the scrap heap."

"Don't go making insulting remarks about my trusty Toyota. I admit it's got a spot or two of rust, but it still runs like a dream."

"A pretty noisy dream. You can hear it coming a half mile away."

"You can not!"

"Here's how you look for material on arson," said Daisy, tapping on keys. "We don't have a lot, but we have some."

Sure enough, some titles and numbers appeared on the screen.

Magic.

"We're part of CLAMS, too," said Daisy, "so if there's something you want that we don't have here, we might be able to get it for you."

"Clams," I said.

She looked up at me, saw the ignorance in my face, and smiled in a matronly way. "CLAMS is short for Cape Libraries Automated Materials Sharing. It's a consortium. We can get materials from the other libraries in the system. It's right there on your library card, J.W.!"

I looked at my card. She was right!

"Thanks," I said. "I'll start with what you have here. I don't know enough yet to know what I want to know."

"Would Diana like something?"

"She doesn't read much yet, but she likes books with pictures. I'll find some for her."

"Fine. If you need any help, let me know." Daisy went off.

I found books for Diana and for myself, then found chairs for the two of us, and read what there was to read. The arson collection at the Edgartown Library wasn't extensive, but it was enough for a start.

As I already knew, the average cop or fireman lacks the expertise to investigate suspected crimes of arson. On the other hand, I now read, most arsons were pretty amateurish, so were fairly easy to identify as such. Clues apparent even to ordinary folks like me included the presence of flammable liquids, indications that the fire started in several places at once, and the intensity of the blaze. Once the clues were spotted, the experts had to be called in to interpret them because, after that, arson investigation was highly complex and technical.

It got more complicated when death was involved. Having seen one fatality from burning when I worked in Boston, I was aware of the classic pugilistic attitude assumed by the victim's body, but now I learned that Frank Costa had been right about it being due to a contraction of the muscles because of heat. Whatever the cause, it wasn't a sight or a scent that I wanted to experience again.

Most deaths by fire were, as I'd thought, caused by the inhalation of noxious gases and fumes, and the victims were usually dead prior to any burning of their flesh.

After the discovery of a body in a burned-out building, the arson investigators had to determine whether the death was natural, accidental, suicidal, or homicidal. The body might be burned so badly that they couldn't tell whether it was a man or a woman, and it might show violent injury or even dismemberment, so arson investigators relied on pathologists to make determinations as to the cause of death.

Pathologists could determine such things as whether the victim was dead or alive before being burned, and the probable cause of death. Since bodies don't burn as easily as most people believe, it was possible for a pathologist to discover wounds or injuries in spite of damage to the body caused by fire. If, for instance, the victim was still alive at the time of the fire, there would be smoke stains around the nostrils, in the nose, and in the air passages. There would be carbon monoxide in the blood, and blistering of the skin. All bodies, whether alive or dead at the time of the fire, could show similar characteristics: the pugilistic stance that I had seen, cracked skin, broken bones, or cracked or shattered skulls.

Increasingly, according to my grim and grisly book, arson investigators were obliged to call in homicide detectives to aid in their investigations. This was true, apparently, because the combination of homicide and arson was becoming more common as killers used arson as a murder weapon or tried to cover up their murders by torching their victims and the scenes of their crimes.

What a way to make a living. I felt sorry for the pathologists and fire marshals, and I was gladder than ever that I had left the policeman's life behind me. Better by far to be a fisherman on Martha's Vineyard.

I looked down at little Diana, who was peering seriously at pictures of the Cat in the Hat. If she grew up and wanted to become an arson investigator or a homicide detective, I guessed I wouldn't try to stop her, but I'd surely suggest some other careers. Maybe she could write and illustrate books about, say, the Rat in the Hat, or the Bat in the Hat. Yeah, that sounded good. Diana could become a rich and famous writer and would support her ma and pa in regal fashion, as they deserved.

Meanwhile, I had learned as much about arson as I could stand for the moment, so I pushed my books away, and went to see if I could find out anything about Corrie Appleyard. There were books about music and musicians, but if Corrie was mentioned in any of them, I didn't notice it. Rats. I went back to my table, sat down beside Diana and the Cat in the Hat, and looked around. A mild surprise. There, on the far side of the room, elbows on a table, poring over a book, was Warren Quick.

It was a weekday, but Warren, who had the reputation of working every day but Sunday, wasn't working. He was at the library, reading. Susanna was not in sight. I let my eyes linger on him in idle curiosity. Why was he in here instead of out there? What was he reading that so occupied his attention?

It occurred to me that I was being rather odd in my thinking. Why shouldn't Warren be in the library, reading instead of building somebody's house? I was in the library, reading instead of building the wing on my own house, wasn't I? I loved coming to the library, didn't I? Maybe Warren did, too.

However, this library was a long way from Warren's home. About as far as you could get from Chilmark and still be on the island, in fact. All of the island's town libraries— the Chilmark library, the West Tisbury library, the Aquinnah library, the Vineyard Haven library, and the Oak Bluffs library—were closer to where he lived and worked.

But Warren was at the Edgartown library.

Maybe he had a job in Edgartown and had ducked in here to do some research, or just to relax.

I wondered some more about what he was reading. Whatever it was, it seemed to interest him considerably. My nose began to itch, as it does more often than it should.

I went back to my abandoned book and pretended to read more about arson and homicide while peeking over the top to keep an eye on Warren.

When I got tired of that pretense, I offered to read *The Cat in the Hat* to Diana, who immediately accepted the offer. I read in a low voice, but not so low that Diana couldn't hear me and correct my mistakes when I missed a word or skipped a page because I was paying more attention to Warren than to Dr. Seuss. Diana had *The Cat* memorized and didn't tolerate any lapses by her readers.

By happy chance, Warren finished his reading, got up, and left the library just about the time I was finishing *The Cat*. I was glad to see that he was following library policy by leaving his book on the table instead of trying to return it to its proper place on the shelves. Librarians discourage patrons from returning books where they found them because they all too often return them to some other place, thus effectively losing the book. In really big libraries, such a misplaced book can be lost for years, I've been told.

So Warren had done the right thing, as might be expected. Good old ethical, straight-arrow Warren.

"Stay here," I said to Diana. "I'll be right back."

I walked across the room to the place where Warren had been sitting and picked up his book. It was a book on abnormal psychology. I looked through the table of contents and saw that it dealt with lots of categories, and once again wondered if there were such a thing as normal psychology, and if anyone had ever written a book about it. Probably not.

I put the spine of the book on the table and let it fall open. It opened to a section on sexual deviance.

Hmmmm.

I flipped through the pages. There were a lot of sexual practices that the author considered deviant. I wasn't sure he was right about any of them being abnormal, because all of them seemed to be practiced fairly regularly by someone or other. One of the things I'd learned while on the Boston PD was that people would pay for sexual practices that I had never even imagined.

I wondered which practices interested moral Warren, the churchgoer. Had Warren gotten wise to the fact that his wife had once been in the adult-movie business? Was he trying to understand her? Or had he gotten wind of her blackmailer, and was he trying to understand *him*?

Or was he trying to understand himself, as many people are? Did Warren have impulses and desires that disturbed him enough to lead him to the research shelves? It's often been observed that psychology students are wackier than most other people, or at least they are afraid that they are. Maybe solid churchgoers like Warren were particularly fearful about being sinners.

Or maybe Warren hadn't been reading that portion of the book at all. Maybe it just happened to fall open to that chapter.

I noted the name of the book, closed it, and left it on the table. I could come back and read it if I wanted to. On balance, I preferred *The Cat in the Hat*, so I checked that one out when Diana and I left and headed for home.

15

Zee and Joshua were just sitting down to lunch. We joined them. Gazpacho and ham sandwiches made with home-made white bread. Delish! Like their parents, Joshua and Diana would eat almost anything, even good food, so we had no cater-to-the-kids problem.

"Well?" said Zee, dishing out the gazpacho for her rav-enous offspring.

It was only noon but it already seemed like I'd put in a full day. I munched a mouthful of sandwich and swal-lowed, then told Zee what I'd been up to. Except for Judith Gomes's arson threat. I rarely tell anybody everything. In this case, I didn't want Zee to worry for no good reason. She had enough on her mind, what with having a steady job, two little kids, and a husband like me.

"So now what?" asked Zee, interested in where my inquiries were taking me in spite of her dislike of the idea that I was working for Ben Krane.

"I want to see Jack and Sandy Dings, the arson investi-gators, in case they know something I can use or I know something they can use. And I'm going to call Quinn."

"Quinn? What about?"

Quinn was a reporter for *The Boston Globe*. We'd met and hit it off when I was working in Boston, as cops and reporters sometimes do, and had remained friends ever since.

"I want to get information on Corrie Appleyard. I didn't find any in the library, but Quinn will know how to get it. You know Quinn. He's got a nose for news."

The mention of Corrie's name created a momentary

silence at the table. Then Zee said, "I wonder if that was really him in the house."

But both of us, I thought, believed that it was.

"We'll have to wait for the report from the medical examiner," I said.

She nodded. But then, being a nurse, who like other nurses had seen more death and damaged bodies than most people do, she shook off her melancholy and moved on. "What do you want to know about Corrie?"

"I don't know, but I want to know all I can."

"But if that's him, he's just a victim. He didn't start the fire."

"I know. But I still want to learn what I can."

She nodded. "I know how your brain works. You think the past is prologue."

She was right, of course. I usually do think that. Coincidence happens, but it's more likely, I think, that our fates are rooted in our past actions, our dispositions, our habits. Our futures are decided because of who we are and what we do, how we live and who we know, more than by simple happenstance, although fortuity plays its part. Our fates, dear Brutus, as Old Bill might have written, lie not in chance, but in ourselves.

"If nothing else," I said, "I'd like to know if Corrie has a family. I have his guitar out in the truck, and it should go to his kin, if he has any. Quinn can find info on Corrie, if there's any to find."

"If you want to know about Corrie, there's another person you might ask," said Zee between slurps of gazpacho.

"Who?"

"Cousin Henry Bayles."

Cousin Henry Bayles. Last seen being embraced by Corrie after the concert in the church.

"Cousin Henry is not known for answering questions," I said. "They say that reporters tried to interview him when he first came to the island, and he threatened to loose his dog on them. I think he still has that dog."

"Well, he and his wife and Corrie seemed pretty close, and friends know about friends, so maybe he knows Corrie's family, too."

"Sound reasoning, except for the fact that Cousin Henry doesn't take to strangers asking him questions."

"You're not quite a stranger."

True. I'd once talked with Cousin Henry for about twenty minutes and had lived to tell the tale.

"I think I'll save Cousin Henry till last," I said. "I don't want to stretch my luck."

"Pa and I had ice cream," said Diana to Joshua.

Women! They talk when they shouldn't and don't when they should! Joshua looked at me with big eyes. I looked at Zee, who took a bite of sandwich and said nothing.

"Don't worry," I said to Joshua. "You can go with me this afternoon and we'll get you some ice cream, too."

"I want some more," said Diana.

"I'll get some and bring it home and we can all eat it later," I said.

"You're an easy mark," said Zee. "These two have you wrapped around their fingers."

"Piff. I'm hard as nails."

Zee shook her head and smiled a womanly smile.

After the table was cleared, I called Quinn from the bedroom phone. I got his answering machine. What a world. I told the machine who I was and what I wanted and hung up. I'd barely gotten out of the room when the phone rang. It was Quinn.

"What do you want to know about Corrie Appleyard, and why do you want to know it?"

"You sound like you recognize the name. I didn't know you were a blues fan."

"I'm a little bit a fan of the blues, but, more important, I am a knight of the keyboard, a member of the fourth estate. I'm supposed to know things. Besides, when I was a kid reporter I covered a couple of his gigs in Boston clubs. What's your interest in him?"

"I think he may have just died in a fire down here in Paradise."

I could almost see his ears perk up. "Whoa! Died in a fire, eh? Gimme the details."

"Don't get in an uproar, Quinn. I said I *think* he may have died. The official report from the medical examiner hasn't come in yet, so the ID of the body isn't certain. If Corrie shows up, you don't want to be the guy who announced his death."

"But you think it's him. Give me the story."

So I told him about Corrie coming to the island and giving the concerts, and I told him about the fires that were turning Ben Krane's houses into piles of rubble.

"Got yourself an arsonist, too, eh? Better and better." Quinn was already writing his lead in his mind. "Maybe I can get the boss to send me down there. I could stand some time on the island. Are the bluefish still around?"

"They're still around, but before you con your boss into letting you come down here on company time, I need to have you dig up everything you can about Corrie Appleyard."

"Why?" asked Quinn. "Or is that a secret?"

"It's no secret," I said, and told him about my job with Ben Krane.

"Sticking your nose where it doesn't belong again, eh? You should have stayed a cop. Maybe you'd have become a real detective instead of just pretending."

"No insults, Quinn, or I'll make you take care of both my kids the next time you come down."

Quinn had women in his life, but no children that I knew of. Now he feigned horror. "Oh, no, not that! Not both of your little angels at once! I have a better idea. You take care of the kids and I'll take Zee out and show her what a fine time she can have with a real man. She'll thank us both. Incidentally, how's the new wing coming along?"

"It's coming. It'll be done by fall."

"You should be working on that instead of playing

gumshoe, because the quicker you get it done, the quicker the kids will have their own rooms, and the quicker you'll have a guest bedroom again where Brady and I can bunk while Brady chases bass with his fly rod and I romance Zee the way she deserves to be romanced."

"You wouldn't know what to do with a real woman, Quinn, but I'll let you know when the kids are out of the guest room. You really think you might come down for this arson story?"

"There are worse places to work than Martha's Vineyard in the summertime when the bluefish are still around. But before I come, I'll dig up what I can find about Corrie Appleyard. You after anything in particular?"

"No. But if you can find his family, that would be good, because I have his guitar and it should go to them. And the medical examiner can probably use any dental records you can track down."

"Anything else?"

"No. I'm just nosing around."

"I'll be in touch. Thanks for the tip on the story."

"Think nothing of it. A free press is the best defense against tyranny."

"How true." He hung up.

I went out into the yard, where Zee was playing patty-cake with our children.

"How's Quinn?"

"He sends you a leer. He wants me to give up the job with Ben Krane and finish the addition so he and Brady Coyne can come down and sponge off us."

"That sounds like Quinn, and I think he's got the right idea. You should take his advice."

"This job may not take long, and I can use the money for building materials."

"I've got money."

"So do I, although not much. But your money and my money are already allocated, so Krane's money will help."

Her voice was getting more and more crisp. "I can unallocate some of mine, if that's what it takes to keep you from working with Ben Krane."

I looked down at her. Her face was angry, and the sight of that anger angered me.

"What is it about Ben Krane that sets you off?"

"Ben Krane is a vile man!"

"His secretary thinks he's a saint!"

"Ask her if she still feels that way in a year!"

"She's been working for him for six years and she still thinks he's God!"

Zee got up and brushed at her shorts. "She must be a slow learner." She walked into the house.

I felt arms around my leg and looked down at Diana.

"Play, Pa."

"No," said her brother. "Pa's getting ice cream with me." He put his arms around my other leg.

Family discord in both generations, and no solution in sight. Ye gods!

I knelt and took Diana's hands in mine. "Joshua's right. I told him I'd get ice cream for him just like I got it for you this morning. I'll bring more back when we come home, and we can all have some after supper."

So the male Jacksons, one full of discontent, drove away, leaving the female Jacksons, both full of discontent, at home. Justice is elusive in this world, as any woman will tell you.

— 16 —

First things first: a quick trip into town to get ice cream. More black raspberry for me, strawberry for Joshua. I am an ice cream fan, and always enjoy it when I eat it, but for some reason rarely get around to buying any unless urged to do so by my children, who love it greatly and request it almost every time we go into any of the Vineyard's villages.

When he was finished with his cone, Joshua wiped his own face fairly well. He was getting better at the job as he grew up.

"How was it?" I asked him.

"Good."

"We'll get more later to take home. But first I have to talk to some people."

"Okay, Pa." He took my hand. His was a bit sticky. We walked to the truck and I strapped him in and we drove to Arbutus Park, listening to the classical station from the Cape. They were playing something that sounded Haydn-ish. They don't get better than Papa Haydn, who must have inspired Mozart, Beethoven, and everybody else who came after him. I wondered what it was like to be a genius. I would never know.

The sour smell of burning was still in the air as we approached the ruin of Ben Krane's latest incinerated house. A burned building never smells sweet and sharp like fireplace smoke or the smoke of burning leaves in the fall; its odor is rancid and foul. Probably because of the insulation, furniture, and other stuff that goes up with the structure.

Goes up. I pondered once again the endless up/down colloquialisms in our language: A stream dries up, never down, but we can drive up or down a street; people can be asked to shut up, but never to shut down; engines start up and shut down; buildings are boarded up, never down; and businesses are closed down and opened up; we come up with ideas, but come down with sicknesses. Up and down.

Houses burn up and burn down at the same time, but the things inside of the houses, both the inanimate and animate, never burn down; they always burn up. Because they have souls, maybe?

I don't believe in souls, but I thought of the burial of Beowulf, and of how the smoke from his funeral pyre rose to the sky, carrying his soul to that heavenly Geatish great hall where heroes live forever. Maybe there was a big nightclub up there where musicians plied their trade for eternity, and maybe Corrie Appleyard was there right now with his mystic guitar, singing the heavenly blues, if there was such a thing.

I pulled off the dirt road and parked not far from the blackened remains of the house. There was a police car parked ahead of me and I saw Sergeant Tony D'Agostine of the Edgartown PD standing by the house with a man wearing boots, helmet, and a long yellow coat. A woman similarly garbed was not far away, holding a clipboard and writing something.

"Stay here," I said to Joshua.

"I want out," he said.

"Stay here for now. There's a lot of broken glass around, and I don't want you to get hurt."

"I won't get hurt."

"Stay. I'll be right back. If it looks safe, you can get out." I turned the key so the music would play from the radio. "Meanwhile, listen to this. It sounds like Vivaldi. Vivaldi is always good."

I got out and walked over to Tony. He nodded.

"I'm looking for Jack and Sandy Dings," I said.

The man in the helmet said, "I'm Dings." He was a tall man who looked to be about fifty years old, although these days I have a hard time telling how old anybody is. The young kids want to look like adults and the adults want to look like kids. Dings looked like an adult.

"J. W. Jackson," I said. We shook hands. His was sooty, like his face.

"What can I do for you?" asked Dings.

"I've been hired by the guy who owns this place," I said. "He wants me to find out who's torching his buildings. I was hoping you and I might work together."

Dings's face became expressionless. "Are you a private arson investigator of some kind, Mr. Jackson?"

"No. I'm not a private investigator of any kind. I'm just a civilian."

The woman came over. "I'm Sandy Dings," she said. "I'm afraid this isn't a civilian job, Mr. Jackson."

"You may be right. For sure, I don't know a thing about arson."

"Then you'll probably just be in the way," said Jack Dings. "I suggest that you go back to your boss and tell him I said to leave this investigation to professionals. When we know what happened here, we'll let him know."

"That's what I told him when he hired me, but he hired me anyway."

Sandy Dings's eyes were hard. "Doesn't trust the fire marshals, eh?"

"I don't know who Ben Krane trusts, but he wants to find the guy who's torching his places, and he's paying me to do it."

"Well, you won't be getting much information from us. When our report is done, we'll give it to our boss and he'll probably give it to yours. We won't have much to say until then. Now, if you'll excuse us." They both turned away.

"If you won't give me any information, maybe I can give you some. Has the body been identified yet?"

They turned back. "Do you know who it was?" asked the woman.

"No, but I can make a guess. I think it was a man named Corrie Appleyard. He was staying at the house, but supposedly had left the island on the seven-thirty boat, before the fire started."

Jack Dings looked at me. "What makes you think it was him?"

"Because I found his guitar leaning against that tree over there. Corrie was a musician. I don't think he would have left his guitar behind if he was going off island."

"You took the guitar?" His voice became cold. "That wasn't too smart. You tampered with evidence, Mr. Jackson. I think you're in trouble. Where's the guitar?"

"Right over there in my truck."

"Give it to me."

"Sure."

He followed me to the Land Cruiser and I gave him the case. "I'm trying to track down his family," I said. "I imagine they'll want that when you're through with it."

"Show me where you found this."

"Pa," said Joshua, "is there glass?"

I had almost forgotten Joshua. "Not too much. Just be careful where you walk." I turned off the radio and got him out of his seat belt. "This is my son, Joshua," I said to Dings. "Shake hands, Joshua."

Joshua shook Dings's sooty paw and said, "How do you do?" Dings, slightly off balance, said, "Hello."

"And that's his wife, right over there," I said. "Now stay away from the house and watch out for glass on the ground." Joshua wandered off, looking at things that little kids look at.

"Come on," I said to Jack Dings, and took him to the tree where I'd found the case. "It was right here, with a moped."

"You should have left it right where you found it."

"Don't be so sour. You'll notice that the moped is gone. If I'd left the guitar, it'd probably be gone, too. People scrounge around after a disaster; you know that. They don't think of it as looting, they think of it as salvage. The moped belonged to a kid named Adam Washington, who was staying here. He probably came by and took off to wherever he's staying now. It was probably the only thing of his that was saved."

Dings just grunted, but it seemed to me that he wasn't as angry as he had been before.

"What I'm wondering," I said, "is why the guitar case was out here, but Corrie's satchel wasn't."

"Maybe because there was a satchel beside the body," said Sandy Dings, who had come over. "You sure this was Appleyard's guitar?"

"I'm sure."

"You a friend of his?"

"He and my father knew each other years ago when my dad was with the Somerville Fire Department. I met him again earlier this week; it was the first time I'd seen him in about thirty years. He was on the island to give a couple of concerts, and he came by our place because he and my dad used to batch there a long time back. He didn't know my dad was dead."

Jack Dings frowned. "Jackson . . . When I was just getting started in the department, I knew a Rosy Jackson in Somerville. Later he had a wall fall on him during a warehouse fire."

More evidence that the world is small and that we should always watch our language because we never know who we might be talking to. "That was my father," I said.

He studied me. "Now that I think about it, when I look at you I can see the resemblance. Your old man was good at his work. He wasn't on the arson squad, but he probably could have been. He was a pro. You say you're getting in touch with this Appleyard fella's family?"

"No, but a reporter I know in Boston is looking into it for me. Was there anything in that satchel you found? An address book or some such thing?"

"There wasn't much left of it," said Sandy Dings, "but maybe the lab can come up with something." She turned and looked at the remains of the house. "Fire started in the wiring, looks like. No accelerants involved as far as I can tell. The wiring in these old houses is pretty bad a lot of times. We have more checking to do."

"You know that this is the third house belonging to Ben Krane that's burned this year?"

"Yeah," said Tony D'Agostine. "I told them that first thing. Like it said in the old James Bond book, once is happenstance, twice is coincidence, three times is enemy action."

I hadn't pegged Tony for a literary man.

"I agree," I said.

Sandy Dings shrugged. "Could be. The fire last spring was definitely arson, according to what I hear. We didn't handle that job, but now we'll be taking a good look at the records and I'll talk with the investigator." She squinted at me. "Your boss; what kind of a guy is he, if you don't mind me asking?"

"I don't mind. I'm working for him, but I'm not his guardian angel or his PR man. My wife doesn't like him, but hasn't told me why. His secretary lauds him to the sky, but the lady doth praise too much, methinks. He has the reputation of being a sharp businessman, a slumlord, and a lawyer who specializes in defending perps who belong in jail."

"Amen to that last," said Tony. "First, he runs a bail bondsman service, and he's got them out on the street again almost before we can get them in. Then in court the average cop and assistant DA aren't up to his kind of snuff, and the guilty walk. It's enough to make you give up the law-and-order business."

Sandy Dings listened to this, then looked at me again. "Is he the type to torch his own places?"

"If he's burning down his own places, why did he hire me to find out who's doing it?"

"Because he may figure that'll put us on some trail other than his. Maybe you're supposed to drag a red herring over his tracks."

"You mean because I'm an amateur and don't know what I'm doing."

She nodded. "Worse yet, an honest amateur. You'll work hard but all you'll really find out is nothing. And while you're at it, you'll get in our way enough to keep us from nailing him, if he really did it."

It was possible. "Well, I'll try to stay out of your way," I said.

"Don't just try. Do it."

I nodded. "I'm going to talk to some people who know Ben better than I do. If I learn anything, I'll let you know."

"I'd be happier if you'd keep out of the whole business," said Jack Dings. He studied me. "But you're not going to do that, are you?"

"No."

"I didn't think so."

"Well," said Tony. "That being the case, J.W., you should talk with Ben's ex-wives. They should have some opinions about him. See his brother, too. Maybe Peter Hot-Pants can give you some skinny on Ben. They're close, I understand."

"You're a mind reader as well as a member of the literati," I said to him. Then I looked at the two Dingses. "Like I said, if I learn anything, I'll let you know."

"Do that," said Jack, "but don't get in our way or tamper with any more evidence, or I'll have officer D'Agostine here toss you into the hoosegow and you'll have to get your boss to bail you out."

I rounded up Joshua, who had managed not to damage himself or anything else while on the loose, and went back to the truck.

So far I hadn't done much to earn Ben Krane's money. So far, of course, I didn't actually have any of Ben Krane's money.

I headed back downtown.

— 17 —

Ben Krane's first wife, Elaine, still lived in Edgartown. She was remarried and had three teenaged kids. Her husband was another of the island's builders, who make up about 49 percent of the Vineyard's permanent population, and sell their wares through another 49 percent who are in the real estate business. The remaining 2 percent of the island's citizens do everything else. Elaine was one of the 2 percent. She worked in the town hall.

I found her in her office, surrounded by piles of paper. All of the people who work in the town hall are surrounded by piles of paper. The same is probably true of all of the people who work in all of the town offices in all of the towns in the world. And since the invention of computers, I'm told, the situation is worse than ever. The more computers, the more paper. If I had any sense, I'd invest my money, if I had any money, in paper stocks.

I was glad to see that she was alone.

"What can I do for you, J.W.?" she asked, seemingly glad to temporarily stop whatever work she'd been doing when I came in. "Is this your boy?"

"It is. Joshua, say hello to Mrs. Simmons."

He did that, taking her hand in his and giving it a solemn shake.

Elaine smiled at him, then at me. "What are you doing downtown on a nice day like this, J.W.? I'd have thought you'd be fishing or clamming far from the madding crowd."

I decided to get right to the point. "Your ex has hired

me to find out who's burning down his houses. I hope you can tell me something that might help me do the job."

She tipped her head to one side and the smile faded. "Is somebody burning down his houses?"

"So it seems. Or so he thinks, anyway."

"Or so he says he thinks." She smiled a thin smile.

"What do you mean?"

She shrugged. "Oh, nothing. Never mind."

There were two chairs on my side of her desk, and I sat Joshua and me in them. "I don't think it's nothing," I said. "Does Ben say things he doesn't mean?"

Again the shrug. "Maybe he should get the benefit of the doubt. Maybe he's changed in the years since I was married to him."

"If I can't believe what he tells me, maybe I shouldn't work for him."

"Maybe you shouldn't." She touched the papers she'd pushed aside, which I took as an indication that she didn't want to continue the conversation. I thought I'd try to get her interested again.

"Did you hear that another of his houses burned down last night?"

"Of course. This building is a gossip mill. Everybody in it hears everything almost before it happens."

"It's the second house of his that's burned this week, and the third this year."

"Ben never spends a penny on the places. He buys wrecks and lets them fall down even further. It's a miracle more of them haven't burned!"

It was a popular idea. "Did you hear that they found a body in this last building?"

Sympathy replaced the sarcasm in her voice. "Yes, I did hear that. Poor soul. One of the kids who lived there, I imagine."

"I don't think so," I said. "I think it was a friend of mine, a guy named Corrie Appleyard."

"Oh! I'm sorry, J.W.!"

And she was, too, because she was a kind woman. It was the response I'd been hoping for, because her sympathy for me swept away her hostility to my questions.

"Corrie was a good man, so I have a personal reason for wanting to find the arsonist, if there is one," I said. "Maybe you can help me."

"I can't imagine how." Her voice was uncertain but no longer antagonistic.

"I'm not sure, either, but the more I know, the better. One possibility is that the arsonist is angry with Ben for some reason. I don't know Ben well, but you do. You were married to him."

Her face became cautious again. "That was a long time ago. We were both just kids. We never should have gotten married at all."

"Tell me about him. You've already suggested that he's not completely honest. He's both a lawyer and a business-man. If he makes it a practice to be dishonest with his clients, revenge might be a motive for the fires."

She pursed her lips. "I don't know much about his businesses, I'm afraid. He's very bright and very slick and very successful. I do know that much."

I looked at that ironic mouth and saw that she wasn't really talking about Ben's professional life. She seemed to be thinking backward through time.

"Are you talking about the way he treated you?"

She nodded. "And other women. He knows a lot about women. What they want. How to use them. How to juggle several at once and keep each one of them ignorant of the others." She seemed past self-pity.

"Is that why you left him? Because of other women?"

"I probably knew about them earlier than I thought I did. Not even Ben can keep all of the balls in the air all of the time. From time to time he drops one, either by acci-dent or, more likely, on purpose. Some of them bounce, and some of them just roll away into corners. Some of the bouncers talk. Some of them talked to me."

"To warn you or to get back at him?"

Again, that characteristic shrug of the shoulders. "Either. Both. The point is that they let me know what was going on. When I confronted Ben, he denied it at first, then said it would never happen again, all in that bright, sincere way he has when he's lying. After a while, though, I saw through him and left him. Looking back, I wonder why I stayed so long."

"You were pretty young."

"I suppose that might explain it."

"Do you know the names of any of the women who were involved with him?"

"I do, but I don't think I'll give them to you. It all happened a long time ago, and I don't think any one of them is an arsonist."

I thought I knew the name of one of the women. "How about their husbands or boyfriends?"

"Sorry, J.W. You'll have to get that information from someone else. Those dogs are sleeping. I won't wake them up."

I considered that, then nodded. "I don't blame you." I got up and took Joshua's hand. "Thanks for your help."

"If it *was* help. I'm sorry about your friend."

"Thanks. Do you know where I can catch up with Laura?"

"Ben's second marital failure? She lives up in Chilmark, but works in OB in Gussie's Gifts." Elaine smiled a real smile. "You know Gussie Goldman?"

"No. Is she the one Laura left him for?"

"She's the one. Ben's had hard luck keeping wives."

True. First Elaine had left him and found herself another man, and then Laura had left him for another woman. Even Ben occasionally joked about it, I was told.

Elaine was watching us as we went out the door.

Gussie's Gifts was about midway down Circuit Avenue, Oak Bluffs's main drag.

I found a parking place over on Ocean Avenue, and Joshua and I walked back to Circuit, passing the new brew bar on Kennebec Avenue, where they made and served the Vineyard's best draft beer. Brew bars and the microbreweries that are springing up all over the United States are persuasive evidence that the world is not going to hell, as often seems the case, but is, in fact, improving daily. For as the poet observed, malt does more than Milton can to justify God's ways to man.

I found Gussie's Gifts and we went in. A couple of instantly identifiable tourists were fingering merchandise. Elderly ladies just off the tour bus that had circumnavigated them around the island, I guessed. Their busy fingers lifted objects up toward their eyes and put them down again, then moved on. When the ladies returned over the water to the mainland, they could tell their less traveled friends all about the Vineyard while showing them the evidence from Gussie's Gifts that they actually had been there.

The shoppers were being casually but carefully watched by an informally but neatly dressed woman behind the counter, and I wondered how much merchandise such nice little blue-haired ladies managed to pilfer from shops every year. It probably came to a goodly amount, I imagined, since I've never seen much evidence that we get more honest as we get older.

I went to the counter and the woman smiled at me. She had an intelligent face under curly hair held back by a scrimshaw comb. I told her I was looking for Laura Krane.

"Laura is working out back. Let me call her."

"It's a personal matter, not business. Maybe I should wait until she takes a break. I won't need much of her time, in any case."

She gave me a fast study. "Why don't you just go on back. She's right through that door."

I led Joshua into the back room and found another woman unpacking ceramic lighthouses from a carton that had come from Hong Kong. She was one of those people who are medium: medium height, medium weight, medium face, medium everything. No distinguishing marks, I first thought. But then I saw that I was wrong. Her eyes, behind large glasses, were full of life and humor. I gave her my name and Joshua's name and told her I was looking for Laura Krane.

"I'm Laura Krane."

I told her about my job and hoped that she might be able to help me by telling me anything about Ben Krane's life or character that could perhaps point me toward a possible arsonist.

She laughed. "I'm afraid I can't tell you much about Ben, Mr. Jackson. I wasn't married to him very long."

"But you were married to him for a while, so you must have some thoughts about him."

She unwrapped another ceramic lighthouse. It looked somewhat like the East Chop lighthouse, and had the words "Souvenir of Martha's Vineyard" written across its base. She put the lighthouse on a shelf beside some others just like it.

"I married Ben when he was on the rebound after his divorce from Elaine. I think he married me to prove to himself that he was marriage material, just as I married him to prove to myself that I didn't really prefer women to men. Both of us were wrong. We both saw the light in pretty short order. Especially after I met Gussie. Does that shock you, Mr. Jackson?"

"No. I still get shocked by some things, but not by love."

Her smile seemed to light the room.

I said, "Ben thinks somebody's torching his houses. Do you have any idea who might be mad enough at him to do that?"

She dug out another lighthouse. "How about some of the other women he's played around with?"

"Elaine doesn't think any of them are the arsonist type. She wouldn't give me any names."

"Elaine is a nice lady."

"Can you think of any women who might have it in for him?"

"He's left some pretty mad people in his wake, but I don't know of any who'd burn down his houses."

"If there is one," I said, "I think it must be one of his latest conquests, someone he romanced sometime during the last year or two."

"Oh? What makes you say that?"

"Because the fires just started this spring, and I can't imagine some old flame, you should pardon the pun, waiting too long to get even."

"Maybe she was Italian."

"You mean the old saw about revenge being a dish Italians prefer to eat cold. Well, there is that. Most people have hotter heads, though."

"You may be right." She paused. "I haven't kept track of Ben or his women since I left him, so even if I wanted to give you the names of his more recent interests, I'm afraid I couldn't." She paused again, then smiled a sudden smile. "Maybe whoever it is isn't mad at Ben at all. Maybe it's Peter who pissed them off."

"Peter Krane? Ben's brother?"

"Yes. Peter Porn, as he's known to some. He's as kinky as Ben is straight. Supposedly Peter is a very very proper husband to a very very proper wife in New York City, but when he comes to the Vineyard he plays a different role with the local ladies. He specializes in fast romances involving sex games that Ben would never even think of playing."

Peter Porn. I hadn't heard that before. "What kind of games?"

"Slave games. Or so I've been told. I'm just a plain, conventional lesbian, myself, and I don't do slave and master. But I hear that Peter does, and that he's disciplined more than one of Ben's ladies after Ben has moved on. Sort of a brother-helping-brother deal. Good for all involved, as it were. Maybe somebody didn't like what Peter had her do and blamed Ben for it. Crazier things have happened."

True. "I don't suppose you have anyone particular in mind?"

"No, I don't. Why don't you ask Peter or Ben about it? They should know who's maddest at them."

I thought that was good advice. Little half-formed ideas began to flit around through my brain like, yes, bats in a belfry.

"Elaine Simmons told me that you live in Chilmark," I said. "Do you know Susanna Quick?"

She nodded. "Sure. She and Warren live down the road. They're both very nice people. Very respectable. Just like Gussie and me." She grinned.

"I'm hungry, Pa," said Joshua, who never lied about such things. I looked at my watch. It was time to buy ice cream for all of the Jacksons and go home.

I thanked Laura Krane for her time and went out to the street. The two little ladies were still in the store, taking their time about deciding what to buy or steal.

— 18 —

Everybody has a favorite ice cream, so I ended up bringing home four different kinds: black raspberry for me, chocolate chip for Diana, strawberry for Joshua, and coffee for Zee. No one complained that I had gone overboard; in fact, for a while, no one had anything to say at all, for when the Jacksons eat, talk and other considerations are set aside until the food has been consumed.

The midafternoon ice cream break having ended, it was nap time for the small Jacksons, and nearly go-to-work time for Zee, who was on the four-to-midnight shift.

Zee was quiet and seemed almost sad as we sneaked out of the kids' room and left them to sail off in their wooden spoon into the sea of dew. I touched her arm and we went out onto the porch.

"Look," I said, "I know you don't want me to do this job for Ben Krane, but we can use the money. Besides, if that really is Corrie's body, I want to know what happened and how and who, if there is a who. I don't think I'll be on this case for more than a week, so if you can, I wish you'd just put it out of your mind. I don't like this tension between us."

She put her arms around me and laid her head against my chest. "I don't like it either."

I held her against me, feeling relieved. Then she said, "I wish you'd drop the job. Please drop it."

We stood there more like statues than humans, our arms wrapped around figures of stone.

"Why?"

"Because I want you to. Isn't that enough?"

I tried to see into her mind, into her psyche, into her heart, but could perceive nothing that might explain her insistence. It was unlike either of us to ask the other not to do anything that person was set on doing, even if we thought it foolish.

I kissed the top of her head. "I'll think about it," I said. "But while I do, I'm going to try to talk to a couple more people before you go to work."

She stepped away and ran a hand through her hair. "Who?"

"Peter Krane, if I can find him. I think he flies in on weekends, so he may be in town. And I should talk to Susanna Quick about that other matter."

"I wish you'd just do the job for Susanna."

"I know."

"But you'll do what you want. Well, you only have an hour, so you'd better get going."

She brushed by me and went into the house. A weight of woe seemed to push down on my shoulders and it made me both tired and angry. I went out to the Land Cruiser and drove into town.

When Peter Krane came to Edgartown from New York, he stayed in a guest house behind Ben Krane's house in Atwood Circle. I drove there, parked, and then followed the walk that led back into Ben's backyard.

The guest house was small and very private. High fences surrounded the yard, and there were no houses behind or beside the fences. A private driveway led through one fence, and on it was parked a new Jeep with those dark glass windows that let you see out but not in. Those windows are very fashionable but somehow irksome, the way some dark glasses are on certain people. You wonder where the eyes behind the glass are looking. I have a couple of pairs of those glasses myself, of course, and I enjoy being behind them as much as I dislike other people being behind theirs. It was a small perversion, but mine own.

I knocked on Peter's door, wondering what I would find inside. Some naked woman chained to the ceiling, being whipped with a silken lash by a black-hooded Peter Krane? Or was Peter Porn a more benign sort of slave master?

The door opened and Peter stood there, fully dressed and hoodless. He was a younger, more slender version of Ben, with a face slightly softer-looking than his brother's falcon countenance. I could see how he might be attractive to women. Perhaps even very attractive.

"Yes?" His voice was rich and gentle. There was a slight smile on his lips. His eyes were watchful.

I told him who I was and who I was working for, and asked if I could come in. He stepped back and I entered the living room. It was neat and comfortable. I didn't see any handcuffs or leather straps lying around. Krane waved at a chair and I sat there. He sat across from me.

"J. W. Jackson," he said thoughtfully. "I think I've heard the name. How can I help you, Mr. Jackson?" He was one of those people, gurus and their ilk, whose very appearance suggests that they have some secret knowledge the rest of us lack. I hoped it was the knowledge I wanted.

And there was a musical quality to his voice, which made me wonder what sort of melodies he might sing to the women who crossed his threshold. Chain gang songs, maybe? My own singing, such as it was, was done privately, and was limited to oldish folk songs and country-and-western numbers. My technique was simple: if I wasn't sure of the words, I played my guitar louder; if I knew them, I sang louder.

"Your brother thinks somebody is burning down his houses," I said. "He's hired me to track down the arsonist. One possibility is that the guy is motivated by revenge, so I'm asking everybody who knows Ben and his businesses to give me some names of people I can check out."

"And now you're asking me. Why? I live in New York. My brother doesn't discuss his business activities with me. I'm afraid I can't help you."

"You don't know of anybody who might have it in for your brother?"

He spread well-manicured hands. "Not a soul. Sorry. As I say, Ben and I don't discuss his business or mine. I come here to get away from business."

"What kind of business are you in, Mr. Krane?"

He waved one of those graceful hands. "A little of this, a little of that. You know." He smiled a smile that no doubt charmed people other than me. After I had been smiling back at him for a while, he added: "I do a little publishing and I have some interest in movies and theater. My wife likes live theater better than coming down here, so it was cheaper for me to work in the business than to buy her all those tickets!" He laughed a laugh he had no doubt laughed before when he offered that line to a listener.

I was looking into the eyes above his laughing mouth and I didn't see too much humor there. Still, he was a handsome man with theater contacts in New York, which could be a pretty attractive combination to some women, I imagined.

"If you don't know anything about Ben's business, maybe you can tell me something about his personal life. Maybe there's somebody who's got it in for him for some private reason."

His smile faded away. "If so, I don't know anything about it. And if I did, I don't think I'd tell you. Does Ben know you're snooping around asking questions about his private life? I doubt it. I think you'd better go." He stood up and his right hand became a fist for an instant before becoming a hand again.

I pointed to the phone. "Call him. Tell him what I've said here." He hesitated and I put fast words into the pause to lever him away from his refusal to talk to me. "Your brother has given me carte blanche to do this my way, but if you don't want to talk to me, I'll pass that on in my report. Ben might be pretty annoyed if it turns out that you didn't tell me something that might have helped me find an arsonist. He's already lost an office and three other buildings, and there was a body in the third one. Even if they don't try to nail him for torching his own places, he might be charged with negligent homicide if the fire marshal decides the building burned because of some wiring Ben should have had fixed."

Krane wasn't happy, but he sat down again. "All right. Ask me, and if I know something, I'll tell you."

"Does he have any business enemies?"

Krane was sullen. "I told you, I don't know anything about his business."

"He never mentioned some sharp deal he pulled, or some client who blames him for a bad ending in a court case?"

"No. As I told you, I don't come down here to talk business. I come down here to get away from business."

"All right, let's talk about what Ben does for relaxation. He's gone through two wives who have a few nasty things to say about him. What about his other women? Any of them mad enough to torch his buildings?"

"I don't know what you're talking about. Elaine got pissed off because he fooled around a little. So what? And Laura is a dyke, for God's sake. Dykes hate all men. Either one of those bitches would bad-mouth Jesus Christ himself!"

"I hear that Ben's a womanizer who wham-bams them and then drops them without the 'thank you, ma'am.' I hear that there are some mad women out there, and I'm wondering if one of them is pissed off enough to hurt Ben where he's got some real feeling: in his wallet. You know any name that might fit that description?"

"No."

I studied him and let him study me, then I said, "All right, tell me about the women he handed on to you when he was done with them. If they weren't mad enough at him already, maybe they were when they found out he'd sent them to the slave market. Any names of anybody feeling that way come to mind, Peter?"

Anger flared from his eyes, and I thought he was going to come at me. But he caught himself and slowly eased back into his chair.

"I never force anyone to do anything. There's no slavery here."

"You mean that if I get up and wander around this house, I'm not going to find any ropes or tape or cuffs or chains or gags or blindfolds or other toys?"

He studied me. "What if you did? What would that prove?"

"It might prove that you like to play master to women who like to be mastered or who are at least willing to play that game for a while."

"I'll let you in on a secret," he said with a sneer. "There's more of those babes out there than you might think. Besides, there's no law against people doing anything they want as long as they do it in private."

He was technically wrong about that, but I took his point. "I'm not concerned about what consenting grown-ups do with each other," I said, "but I do want to know if Ben or you or both of you have been involved with a woman in the past several months who might be so mad that she'd torch Ben's houses to get even."

He thought about that. "Just the past several months?" He thought some more, then shook his head. "No. Nobody I can think of." Then he smiled a smile that became a grin seen, perhaps, by some of the women he'd brought home: a white-toothed grin that had no pity in it. "You want to go a few years back, I might be able to give you a name or two!"

I didn't like him very much. "Tell me," I said, feeling the anger in my face.

He must have seen it, too, for he was already changing his mind and shaking his head. "No," he said. "No, forget it. I can't remember any names in particular."

"Just being a jackass, eh?"

He came out of his chair like a dancer. I was only a shade slower. Our eyes were about level.

"Get out of here," he said, but my impression was that he was only acting, saying what he thought a tough guy would say.

"What do you do with a woman who doesn't want to play your games?" I asked.

"Get out."

"I imagine that's what you say to them, too."

I suddenly realized that I was hoping he would take a swing at me and felt like a fool. "Never mind," I said. "I can find my way out."

I went past him and out the door. As I did, I heard him say, "Don't come back," and had to force myself to keep walking. Something in us never grows up.

19

Because Zee had to go to work in not too long, I didn't have time to drive to West Tisbury, so I drove to the police station instead. The chief was dealing with a pile of papers. If policemen didn't have to spend so much time doing paperwork and standing around in court waiting to testify, the crime rate in the United States would probably plummet.

"Hi," I said. "Is this what they call protecting and serving?"

"I'm busy," he said. Shuffling paper never put him in a good mood.

"I've been nosing around," I said, "but I'm not getting very far."

"No surprise there. You should leave snooping to us professionals."

I told him who I'd talked to and what little they'd said.

"I wouldn't talk to you either," said the chief. "If I had more energy, I'd throw you out of here right now, in fact."

"You're going to need all of your strength just to file those papers," I said. "I don't suppose you can point me to any angry women who've been cut adrift by Ben or his little brother?"

He studied a sheet of paper and put it on one of the piles adorning the edge of his desk. "If I do know any women like that, I don't plan to tell you or anybody else who they are. They've had enough grief from the Kranes without you giving them more." He opened a file and began to finger through its contents.

I thought that if our positions were reversed, I wouldn't

tell me the names, either. Most people can grow away from their hurts if you let them. Still, I said, "I presume that if you thought any of them were likely arsonists, you'd be checking them out yourself."

"You can presume that I know my job."

In fact, I did presume that. "Don't be in such a snit," I said. "I'm a citizen. I have a right to know that the police I pay for with my taxes are on top of things."

"Take my word for it, citizen Jackson, we are."

"What about Ben's businesses? Any of his scuzzy clients mad at him because he didn't manage to weasel them out of the clutches of the law? Anybody he screwed in a business deal who might torch him because he burned them?"

The chief closed the file and gave me a sorrowful look. "You're a pitiful specimen, J.W. You actually expect me to give you the names of people mad at Ben Krane?"

"It doesn't hurt to ask. Maybe if you give me a lead I can make a citizen's arrest and be a hero."

"And maybe if I grow green hair I can be the King of May."

"I see kids walking around with green hair," I said. "It's not impossible for you to grow some, I suppose, although you're not doing too well lately with the batch God gave you."

"One problem with identifying Ben Krane's enemies is that there are too many of them. He's screwed a lot of people and done it legally. He's a sharp guy, unlike most of the lowlife that I deal with. In fact, I wouldn't be surprised if he screws you on this deal you've got with him. He give you any money yet?"

"The check is in the mail," I said defensively.

He shook his head. "Sure it is. Anyway, Ben is not exactly a beloved figure hereabouts, as you must know. He's lost three properties since spring, and unless he's torching them himself, it seems a hair more than possible that someone else is doing the job. Or it may just be coincidence. The houses were all old and just waiting to catch fire or blow down."

"But you don't believe it was coincidence, do you?"

"Do you?"

"Give me a couple of names."

"No."

"You're a tough one, Captain Bligh. I presume that there'll be an insurance investigator down here sooner or later, to make sure that they don't pay up on something Ben might have burned down himself."

"I believe that's safe to say," agreed the chief.

"If I find out anything, I'll let you know. Unlike some people I know, I'm a cooperative, caring member of our social group."

"Out, out, damned spot. I have work to do."

I went out and drove home.

Zee was in her white uniform when I got there. The contrast between the uniform and her dark, Portuguese beauty was startling, as always. If looks alone could cure, the patients who came to the Emergency Ward would be back on the streets in no time. I put my big hands on her shoulders. "Are you okay?"

She pulled my head down and kissed me. "I'm working on it."

"Can I help?"

"Tell me that you love me."

"I love you."

"Are you quitting this job?"

The weight I'd felt earlier came back. "Not yet."

"I didn't think so." She put her hands up to my face and held it between them. "Are we too much alike, do you think?"

"You mean about being stubborn? Of course not. You're the only stubborn one in the family. I'm flexible as a snake. Wishy-washy, even. Yeah, maybe we are."

"That and not liking other people telling us what to do."

"No, neither one of us is much good at that."

"And not always telling things to each other, even though we love each other."

Yes. "I don't know how much you don't tell me; I only know how much I don't tell you."

She looked up at me with those great, deep, dark eyes and gave my cheek a little pat. "I've got to go. See you later."

I bent down and we kissed again and then she was gone.

I peeked into the kids' room and saw that they were still asleep. It wouldn't be for long, though, so I decided to use my brief time alone to make some calls. The first one was to the Quick Erection Company in West Tisbury. As I'd hoped, Susanna Quick answered from the office.

"This is J. W. Jackson. Can you talk?"

Her voice was agitated. "Yes, I can talk. Warren is out on a job. I'm glad you called. I was just about to call you!"

"Another phone call from your admirer?"

"Yes!"

"Can you talk about it on the phone?"

"I don't want to, but I can."

"Did you recognize the voice? Was it the same person?"

"I think so. I don't know. It's like he's talking through a fog."

"Did he threaten you?"

"Yes! No. He says he wants me to . . . do things that I do . . . that I used to do . . . in the movies. He wants me to do them with him! I told him that I don't do that sort of thing anymore, but he wouldn't listen!"

"Did he ask you to meet with him?"

"No. But he said he knew all about what I'd done, and asked if my husband knew, and I said no, and he said maybe he should know, and then he described some of the things I used to do in Hollywood and said he'd call back soon and hung up."

"Could you trace the call?"

Her voice was apologetic. "No, I haven't talked with the telephone company yet. I know I should have. Maybe I can do it today."

"That would be a good idea. He didn't threaten to hurt you or your family?"

"No, nothing like that. I was an idiot to have made those movies."

"Have you thought any more about telling Warren everything?"

I heard panic in her voice. "Oh, no! I can't do that! He's a wonderful man, but he's, you know, religious and very proper. Why, I was the one who suggested the name for this company, and I honestly think he didn't get the pun until it was too late! I wish now I'd never done that either, but it seems to be helping us get business. People laugh at first, but when they see how fast and how well Warren builds things, they recommend us to their friends. Anyway, I don't want him to know about me before I met him. It would shock him terribly, and I'm afraid of what it might do to our marriage."

I thought of the conversation I'd just had with Zee; of our admission that neither of us told the other everything.

"All right," I said. "You can leave Warren out of things for the time being. Maybe we can pull this off with him never being the wiser."

"Oh, I hope so."

"Do you have any idea at all who this guy might be?"

"No, none. Although . . . sometimes I think I hear something in his voice—not his voice, exactly, because that's always muffled—but something . . . I can't really say what . . . something that reminds me of maybe somebody I do know, or did know. But I can't put my finger on it. Maybe I'm just imagining it. I don't know."

"Do you know a man named Peter Krane?"

A pause. Then, "No, I never heard of him. Who is he?"

"Do you know a man named Ben Krane?"

"Ben Krane, the real estate guy? I've heard of him, but I don't know him."

"They're both womanizers, from what I'm told. The difference is that Ben likes his sex straight and Peter likes his with kinks. Peter works in the theater business in New York City. He's got his hand in movies and publications too, he says. I don't know what sort of material he handles in New York, but here on the island he apparently plays dominance/submission games with women. If his New York work is in the same field, it seems possible that he may have come across the movies you made. I thought if you knew him or had met him here on the island, he might have recognized you and he might be the guy who's been calling you. Are you sure you don't know him?"

"I've heard of Ben Krane, but I don't remember ever seeing him. And I've never even heard of his brother. Do you really think it could be him?"

"Maybe he was a customer who came into the office." I told her what he looked like.

"I don't remember seeing anybody like that." She paused. "But we've done business with a lot of people. Maybe . . ."

"Maybe he bought something," I said. "Will you check your records?"

"Yes. I'll call you if I find anything."

"Good. It's probably not him but if his name's in your books, I'd at least put him on the suspect list. Meanwhile, how gutsy do you feel?"

"Not very, to tell you the truth."

"Okay, but if you change your mind, the next time the guy calls, whoever he is, see if you can arrange a meeting with him. If you can, let me know when and where, and I'll be hidden there when you meet him, if he shows up. Can you do that?"

"Oh, I don't know . . ."

"If you can't, that's okay. But if you can, maybe we can nip this thing in the bud, and Warren won't ever have to know anything about it."

"I'll try."

"Good girl. Don't worry. Mr. Black will be the one who's surprised, not us."

Bold words, for it's not unknown for the ambusher to be ambushed, the besieger besieged.

As I turned from the phone, I wondered how things were going to turn out between Mr. Black and me, and I thought of King Pyrrhus, who came to the oracle seeking foreknowledge of his upcoming battle with the Romans. "Pyrrhus the Romans shall subdue," said the always correct and always ambiguous oracle; it was a prophecy of the original Pyrrhic victory, for though the king won the battle, he suffered such ruinous losses to his own army that he himself was soon overthrown.

Thinking these thoughts, I heard the first sounds of children waking up. It was a sweet sound of stirring and small noises, and as I heard it, my dark musings gave way and I felt blessed.

20

No wonder so few of the detectives in fiction were married and had families. With spouses and offspring and regular jobs taking up all of their waking hours, they wouldn't have time or energy for detecting.

It was the same for cowboy heroes, now that I thought of it. None of them even had jobs, let alone families. They just had horses and skinny bedrolls that supplied them with everything they needed. Where did they get their money, anyway? They never worked for it. They rode into the movie, cleaned out the bad guys, and rode out again. Who fed them? Where did they get their horses? And who paid for all those six-guns and bullets?

Had Hollywood been pulling a fast one all of these years?

It was time for me to talk with my boss, who might be the only person who would tell me about his more serious enemies. No one else would, for sure. I rang his office. Judith Gomes answered in a cheerful voice that immediately grew cold when I identified myself. Ben wasn't in. Yes, she'd have him call me. *Click*.

Click. A lot of people had clicked on me of late, so to speak. Was it my breath?

My daughter trotted out of the kids' room and climbed up into my lap, rubbing her eyes. Her brother came out and got on the other knee. They seemed to like me, even if Judith Gomes and Peter Krane didn't.

"Play with us, Pa."

So I did that until the phone rang. I was the horse and

they were the riders. I bucked Joshua off over my head and caught him before he hit the ground.

"More, more!"

But the horse stood up. "Later. Play by yourselves for a while and don't hurt anybody. Joshua, you're the biggest, so you keep a watch on Diana. Diana, be careful." I went into the house. Ben Krane was on the phone.

I told him who I'd been talking with and more or less what they had declined to say about people who might be so mad at him that they'd burn down his houses. Ben did not seem pleased with my efforts.

"I don't want you nosing around in my private life! Just go out there and find this firebug! Remember, I can fire you any time I want to!"

"We've been over that already," I said. "What you call your private life is exactly where I and the insurance investigator and the fire marshal's office are going to be looking to find out what's going on. You can fire me if you want to, but you can't fire those other guys."

"Stay away from my brother, then! He's got nothing to do with this!"

I was running out of patience with the whole case. "How do you know? Maybe he torched the places himself or hired somebody to do it. You piss him off somehow in the past six months?"

"No!"

I pushed it further: "Maybe one of your discarded women turned out to be tougher than he could handle. Maybe she told him that you laughed about what a punk he is and she decided to rub his nose in it. Most women will only put up with so much before they hit back. A smart one could get both of you with one stone."

"Nobody did anything like that! You start spreading stories about me and my brother and I'll sue your ass to kingdom come!" Lawyer threats were always good.

Almost always. "Sue and be damned," I said, feeling loose and relieved by the prospect that he might actually fire me. "Meanwhile, if you want me to keep working for you, you come up with some names for me to chase down. I'm tired of people telling me what they won't tell me!"

I could almost see him take a deep breath and slowly let it out. "All right, all right, let's both calm down. You say nobody will give you any names, eh? Well, maybe that's because there aren't any names to give. I drive a hard bargain now and then, but I don't cheat anybody."

"I hear differently. I hear that some people think you screwed them royally."

I could hear the sneer. "Some people are born losers. I've never violated a law or an agreement."

"I'm less interested in whether you followed the law than in whether somebody out there hates your guts."

"I don't like that talk!"

"I don't care. Are we going to go on like this, or are you going to give me some names?"

His voice became cautious. "Who do you have in mind?"

"I don't have anybody in mind. That's why I'm talking to you. You tell me whom I should check out."

There was a silence, then, "I can't think of anybody. There are probably a lot of people who don't like me, but I can't think of any who'd set fire to my houses, especially when they're occupied. I don't think I know any murderers."

"What about a husband or boyfriend of one of your women? Any of them ever try to put a fist through your face?"

"Ah." His falcon smile came over the phone into my ear. "Yes, there was one guy like that. He thought his slut had been done wrong. He lost some teeth trying to be Galahad. I think he and the little bitch both left the island. Good riddance."

Ben Krane was one of those people who lived in a world full of sluts, jerks, and bitches. It was a sorry sort of life, I thought. "What was his name?" I asked.

"Let's see . . . I'm not sure I remember. Some common

name. Jones, or Smith, or Johnson. Something like that. I only met him that one time. He came at me in the parking lot, the dumb fuck, shooting off his mouth about what he was going to do to me for damaging his honey. I kicked him in the balls, then, while he was grabbing himself and squealing like a pig, I smashed his face into a car door. Self-defense, and there were plenty of witnesses that he swung first. No charges were filed." Krane laughed.

"What was the woman's name?"

"Linda. She was a looker, but there was nothing to her. She wasn't around me for long."

"You pass her on to Peter Porn?"

He flared. "Don't talk about a member of my family like that!"

I almost laughed. "Or what? You'll fire me? Sue me?"

"That and beat the shit out of you to boot!"

"We have a really great labor-management relationship, Ben. Make up your mind. Am I still working for you or not? It won't break my heart to get through with you and this job."

I could hear what sounded like air being drawn through clenched teeth. Then, "We're too much alike. That's the trouble."

"We're nothing alike. Well?"

"Okay, okay. Take it easy. You're still hired."

"All right. Linda who?"

"Linda Carlyle. You know her?"

I tried to put a face to the name. "No."

"Worked at the Harbor View last year. Waitress. The fighting boyfriend worked in the kitchen. I don't think either one of them lasted the summer. Probably nobody wanted a toothless cook!" Again, Krane laughed.

I clenched my jaw. "They left the island?"

"How should I know? I never saw either one of them after the parking lot bit."

"Anybody else I should track down?"

"Nobody as mad as the boyfriend."

"If I come across any more names, I'll be back to you. I'll expect your check in tomorrow's mail." I hung up before he could say anything else. I could understand why Zee didn't like him much.

Sometimes you can get a lot accomplished over the phone, but not always. I like to keep track of island cooks, because I like to eat and I get some good recipes by being cozy with the pros in hotel kitchens, so I knew Sid Silva, the chef at the Harbor View, and I gave him a call. He was out shopping, and the second in command was new in Edgartown and had never heard of Linda Carlyle. I asked him to have Sid ring me back when he got in.

"Pa, play some more."

"For a while."

"Good. Catch me!"

"Go outside, then. Not in here."

The simple games are the best. We went out into the yard and ran around screaming and chasing and tagging and running away screaming some more until I was worn out. I lay on my back on the lawn and puffed, and the kids, almost too tired themselves, finally came and lay down on top of me, panting.

We looked up at the sky and watched the summer clouds shift shape as they eased downwind. I was actually almost asleep when I heard the phone ringing. I got the kids off me and made it inside in time to answer Sid's fourth ring.

"I hear you were asking about Linda Carlyle. I haven't seen her since last year. She quit working here and went off island."

"She had a boyfriend who worked with you in the kitchen. Do you remember his name?"

"I should. Perry Jonson. He and Linda took off together and left me shorthanded right when things were busy here. Not that I blame him, what with him getting the crap knocked out of him by Ben Krane. You hear about that?"

"I heard. You say they left together? Off island?"

"So I was told. They lived together up in one of those houses in the woods that the college kids rent, then fill up with their friends so they can party and maybe actually save some money, too. Another girl who worked here lived in the same house. She told me they'd gone away and weren't coming back."

"You know where they went?"

"No. Down south someplace, as I recall, but I really don't remember."

"Did they stay away, or did they come back?"

"I never saw either one of them again, is all I can say."

"What was the other girl's name?"

"Peg Sharp. As a matter of fact, she's back here again this year. Damned good waitress. Nice kid, too."

"I want to talk with her."

"Lemme check the work schedules." He went away and came back. "She'll be here tonight for the evening shift, but she'll be busy."

"I only need a few minutes of her time."

"Okay. Come by just before six. She usually gets here a few minutes early. You can talk with her then."

"Great."

At half past five I got the kids into the Land Cruiser and drove into Edgartown. Knowing that the A & P–Al's Package Store traffic jam would have cars backed up for a half mile, I went up to Dodgers' Hole and cut through, along Metcalf's Way, to the West Tisbury Road, where I took a left and went into town the long way roadwise but the short way timewise. The only solution to the A & P traffic jam is to run a cement wall down the middle of the street and prevent all left turns, since left turns are the principal cause of all traffic backups.

I've explained this to the chief and the selectmen time and time again, but does anybody listen to me? No. Just call me Cassandra.

From Main Street I took a left on Pease's Point Way, a right on Morse, and a left onto North Water, where I actually managed to find a parking place right where I wanted one to be.

I got the kids out of the truck, and we walked up to the magnificent and nicely renovated old Harbor View. No one there seemed to care that we were wearing thrift shop clothes, and we went right to the kitchen. It was just before six, and Sid was hard at work with his kitchen crew.

"There," he said, pointing with a spatula at a pretty college-aged woman with her hair firm against her head in those tiny, tight braids that look so hard to make and maintain.

I walked up to her, my children on either side, their hands in mine.

"Peg Sharp?" I asked.

She looked up at me with big dark eyes and nodded. "Yes."

"I'm J. W. Jackson. Do you have a couple of minutes? I want to talk with you about Linda Carlyle."

People were already going into the dining room, but she glanced at her watch and nodded. "Sid said you were coming. The lounge is pretty empty. We can talk there."

I followed her into the lounge.

21

"I don't have long," said Peg Sharp.

"This won't take long. I'm trying to get a line on Linda Carlyle and a guy named Perry Jonson. Do you know where they are?"

"More or less. They're working down in Atlanta for the summer."

"Have they been up here again since they left last year? This spring, maybe, or maybe just lately?"

Anger briefly touched her brown face. "No. They wouldn't come back here. They'll never come back."

"Because of Ben Krane?"

Her eyes became hooded. "I don't know what you mean."

"Yes, you do, Peg. Ben Krane played around with the girl and then tossed her to his brother, Peter, who used her again and got rid of her. Then Ben beat up Perry when Perry went after him. Perry and Linda left here just after that. What I need to know is whether they've been back since."

She seemed relieved to be free of the burden of secrecy. "No. Like I say, they'll never come back here. You know about Peter Krane?"

"I've heard he likes to play dominant/submissive sex games with women, with himself cast as the boss."

"Yeah, well, some women may like that sort of thing, but when he put chains on Linda, it about killed her. It was like slavery was back in fashion, and she was her great-grandma all over again. She fell all apart. There's some psychological term for it, but I forget what it is. When he was through with her, though, she was a total wreck."

"And Perry tried to get back at Ben."

"Yeah. Nice try, Perry, but no go. He was going to get Ben first, then Peter, but he never got past Ben because Ben is some sort of martial arts freak. The two of them smartened up and got away from here. Not that it did Linda all that much good."

"What do you mean?"

Sadness mixed with anger in her voice. "She didn't go back to school. Started taking downers. I think it was to forget, you know? I think most people on downers do it so they can cope."

I shared that view. "Perry wasn't enough for her?"

"Perry means well, but Linda has to be strong in herself, and she hasn't managed that yet. A woman can't expect a man or anyone else to be the strength in her life." Peg Sharp's voice was rich and her eyes flashed.

"Even strong people need a little help sometimes," I said.

"Maybe. I try not to."

I wondered who had hurt her but decided not to ask. "I'd like to talk with them," I said instead. "Do you have an address or a telephone number?"

"No, I don't. Maybe I could get one, though." She looked at her watch, and I knew I'd about used up my time with her.

"Sid said that you and they lived in a house up in the woods last summer."

"Yes, and isn't that an irony! Ben Krane owns the place and that's where he picked her up. She and Perry had had a spat and she was ripe for a smooth older man like Ben. According to what I heard later, Linda wasn't the first woman Ben picked up from one of his own houses. He's a sleaze, but he's a slick sleaze, and he likes to rent to pretty girls who don't mind a summer romance. This year

I made sure I rented from somebody else! Look, I have to get to work. I'll try to get Linda's number for you. If I get it, I'll leave it here with Sid. Okay?"

She edged toward the door, and I stepped aside.

"Three of Ben Krane's houses have burned down since spring," I said as she went past me. "They found a body in the last one."

She gave me a startled look. "Who was it?"

"I don't know for sure. I don't think it was a college kid."

Her expression became one of relief, which quickly changed to cynicism. "I'll bet they have a lot of arson suspects," she said, and went into the dining room.

It's tough to be twenty. Your body will never be better, but your psyche can be pretty fragile.

I went into the kitchen and finally caught Sid's eye. He came over. "I'm pretty busy."

"I can see that. Do you have the address of the house where Linda and Peg lived last year?"

"It's probably written down somewhere, but I don't have time to find it right now."

"I'd like to have it. Maybe you can get it from Peg."

"I'll ring you tomorrow."

"Thanks." He went back to his pots and frying pans, and the kids and I left the hotel.

The lovely Edgartown lighthouse was right in front of us, and since there was nothing else for me to do right then, the three of us walked out to visit it, while admiring the boats already at their moorings and docks, and those coming into the harbor for the night. It was a quiet, lovely scene, far removed from the trouble I was investigating.

Across the outer harbor, where several large power and sail yachts lay at anchor, Chappaquiddick looked peaceful and idyllic in the evening light. The little On Time ferry, so named, some said, because it had no schedule and was therefore always on time, shuttled cars, bikes, and passengers between Edgartown and Chappy. Beyond it, to the west, the June people fished off docks and thronged the streets, ogling the summer sights. Farther still, the masts of other boats were outlined against the hills and houses on the far side of the inner harbor.

It was a lovely sight, but my children were more interested in the shells, stones, and seaweed on the beach. We had a pretty good collection by the time we got back to the truck.

At home, I fixed us a supper of grilled flounder, rice, and pea-pod salad, glad again that Diana and Joshua were, like their parents, pretty omnivorous eaters despite their individual preferences in ice cream. More evidence, perhaps, that I was one of God's chosen? Or was there some other explanation?

Afterward, they got on either side of me on the couch, and I read to them just as my father had read to me long ago. And as he had done for me, I would pause occasionally and point out letters and short words and sound them out. This had helped me start to read when I was four, and since there's nothing better or more fun than knowing how to read, I wanted Josh and Diana to learn how to do it as quickly as possible. As with food, they took to it well. Like dad, like daughter and son. With some of mom thrown in, too, of course.

When they got noddy, I put them in bed and had some time to think grown-up thoughts. I had a lot of them, but they were pretty jumbled; still, it was time to consider them, so I popped a Sam Adams and got to it.

Ben and Peter Krane were sexual predators, but apparently weren't the sort who knocked women around. They were just exploiters and users who liked women as playthings and got bored with them pretty quickly. Linda Carlyle and Perry Jonson were two of their more damaged victims, but there were no doubt others I didn't know about.

Ben liked to rent to pretty girls who might not be averse to summer flings.

He might not punch out women, but he could and

would punch out guys like Perry. And he'd enjoy it. He was a martial arts guy. I didn't know much about the martial arts, but I knew enough to be careful with such people. Most of them were pretty much the same as other people, but there were a few freaks among them, as there are in any group. Freaky martial arts guys were probably a little more dangerous than most other freaky guys. I wondered if Peter was also a martial arts guy. I could ask, if it got to be important.

Three of Ben's houses were gone, and the most recent one had a body in it. I didn't know for sure if there was arson involved or whether the body belonged to Corrie or somebody else, but I *thought* I knew the answers to both questions. Yes, there was arson involved in at least a couple of the fires, and, yes, it was Corrie Appleyard's body.

Because it was Corrie, I had a personal interest in finding out who burned that particular building, if not the others. I was getting paid by a man I didn't care for because I could use the money, but if Ben fired me I'd probably keep hunting on my own, anyway.

Ben claimed he didn't know anyone mad enough to torch his houses, but he could be wrong or he could be lying.

But why would he lie? I couldn't imagine, therefore I should presume he was telling the truth. And since he wasn't stupid, he should know the names of people who had reason to hate him so intensely.

He said he didn't know of any such people, and that the people who disliked him didn't dislike him enough to commit arson.

But if Linda Carlyle was as damaged by the Krane boys as Peg Sharp suggested, she and Perry could be a couple of logical suspects.

But according to Peg, neither of them had ever come back to the island.

But, of course, Peg might not know if they'd come back, or she might be lying to protect her fire-starting friends.

But, but, but, but, but. Lots of *but*'s. Too many.

Maybe I was looking in the wrong places. Maybe I should be poking around somewhere else. But where?

Wouldn't you know: another *but.*

I got on the phone and called Quinn at the *Globe.* He wasn't at his desk. I left a message on his answering machine, asking him how he was doing tracking down Corrie Appleyard's family and history. I tried his apartment. Another answering machine. I left the same message. Everybody in the world but me had an answering machine. Quinn had two, for God's sake. Maybe I should get one. Then my friends and I could have dueling answering machines, and we would never need to talk to one another at all.

I thought about Adam Washington. Where was he staying now? I should try to find out and talk with him. Ditto with Millicent Dowling. She and Adam had had a spat, and I wondered if Millicent could possibly have gotten herself entangled with Ben Krane as a result, the same way Linda Carlyle had done the year before. Ben was always ready for a new woman, after all, and knew how to take advantage of women mad at other men.

Probably not, but it could be.

Had Adam or Millicent been here last summer? Did either of them know Linda Carlyle or Perry Jonson?

I finished my beer and went into the kids' room. They were asleep. I had gotten past my early parental fears that if they were quiet in their beds, it was because they were dead. I got myself another Sam Adams and went up onto the balcony.

The sun had sunk beyond the western brim of the world, and the darkening sky was beginning to fill with stars. The Milky Way crossed above me, high up there in the deep blackness of space. I saw a moving star and knew it was a satellite catching the rays of the departed sun. I watched it cross and disappear toward the horizon. Were there men in it? Or was it all machine? It was lovely, in any case, and I wondered what it was like up there, far, far above this island earth, with its endless ebb and flow of death and desire, ice and fire, joy and despair.

I stayed up there until Zee came home, then I went to bed with her and held her wrapped in my arms until I finally slept.

22

"Definitely arson," said Jack Dings, who was sitting at a table in a room in Oak Bluffs, where he and his wife had been scribbling the first draft of what he identified as their report. "Pretty crude but effective. Old-style fuse box. Guy shut off the electricity, then scraped the insulation off wires leading to a couple of outlets. Then he stuck shiny new pennies under the fuses for those wires and turned on the juice again. Bingo."

Bingo? "Bingo?" I asked.

Sandy Dings nodded. "Normally when there's a short, a fuse blows, but the pennies the guy puts in keep the circuits intact, and bingo. You got yourself two very hot spots in no time at all. Old, dry wood for fuel, plenty of oxygen, and lots of heat. Just what you need for a fire. And since there was nobody around to catch it early, the whole place went up."

"You know yet who the body belonged to?"

She shook her head. "Should know something soon. We're still trying to get a line on that Appleyard guy you mentioned. Dental records, if we can find them."

"If I get any information, I'll pass it along. Is this penny-behind-the-fuse trick an old one?"

Jack Dings looked surprised that I should ask. "Sure, old as fuses and pennies, I imagine. People who blow fuses and don't have extras on hand still do it now and then in their own houses, but it's dangerous as hell."

Such ignorance on my part. It amazed me sometimes that I knew so little of what was common knowledge to others.

"This was an old place," I said. "Maybe Ben Krane's been using pennies for years. Maybe whoever owned the place before Ben bought it used them. Maybe this fire was just the result of criminal stupidity, not arson."

Dings shook his head. "Nope. It's arson, all right."

"How do you know?"

"The pennies are brand new, for one thing, so whoever put them in there did it recently. And the kids I've interviewed have told me Krane hasn't been inside the place for weeks."

"You've been asking them about Krane?"

He gave me an exasperated look. "Of course. Whenever there's arson, the owner is a prime suspect."

"Do you think I'm the only person in the world who didn't know you could use pennies that way?"

"Hell," said Sandy Dings, "it's probably on the Internet, along with a thousand and one other ways to start fires, make bombs, and wreck people's lives and property. Modern communication technology is a wonderful thing."

"If Krane hadn't been inside the house lately, who had?"

Jack Dings smiled a humorless smile. "Well, there's the person we found in the basement, whoever he was. Or she was. And there was the houseful of kids who lived there. And there were their friends and associates who visited them. And there were all of those people who came to their parties. Not more than several hundred folks, all in all."

I had a feeling I didn't like. "Does the lab have what's left of the satchel you found beside the body?"

"Yeah. Why?"

"You might ask them if they found some new pennies inside."

"Oh? Why do you say that?"

"Because when Corrie Appleyard came to visit us, he played some magic tricks with my kids. Pulling coins out from behind their ears, that sort of thing. He used very shiny new pennies."

Both Dingses studied me. "You don't look very happy," said Sandy.

"I'm not. I hope I'm wrong about what I'm thinking."

"And what might that be, aside from the possibility that the body belongs to your friend and the pennies behind the fuses were his, maybe making him the guy who set the fire?"

I don't like it when my emotions start to color my thinking, so I pushed my feelings aside. They didn't want to be pushed. I pushed harder and got them to move back a little, but they didn't leave.

"It's just that if Corrie did scrape those wires and put those pennies in those fuses, it's possible that he learned those tricks from my father, thirty years ago. They used to sit around and drink beer and sing and talk about their work. My father knew as much about fires as Corrie did about the blues, and they were both good listeners."

Jack Dings almost looked sympathetic. "It's a weird world we live in, kid, but I been in this business so long now that nothing surprises me."

It had been a while since anyone had called me kid, and I told him so.

"Don't feel flattered," he said. "Everybody younger than me is just a kid as far as I'm concerned, and that takes in most of the people in the world."

They were back at their work before I even got to the door. Out on the street, I sat in the Land Cruiser for a while, untangling my thoughts from my feelings. I didn't want to find out for sure that Corrie had torched the house and killed himself in the process, and I didn't like the notion that he'd learned the penny trick from my father. The prospect of driving home to Zee and the kids and working on the bedroom wing I was building was a lot more appealing than asking more people more questions about the fires, especially since I didn't like Krane and really didn't care if all of his houses burned down, or up, or both.

Instead, I found a phone and called Sid Silva. He was, as usual, busy. Are chefs in resort hotels ever not busy? "I knew you'd call when I was in the middle of something," he said, "so I brought the address with me when I came to work." He gave it to me. It was for a house that hadn't burned down yet, as far as I knew. I thanked him and told him to go back to his peas and cukes.

Last summer, Peg Sharp, Linda Carlyle, and Perry Jonson had lived in one of Ben Krane's smaller hovels up in the woods near the state forest. I wondered how Krane managed to even find these dumps, but imagined that he, like other foragers for island properties, probably haunted the courthouse and town hall for just such information. Every trade has its tricks, so maybe if I were in the real estate biz I, too, would be alert and aware of its secrets of success. But as things were, I didn't know them, and didn't expect to learn them.

The house was at the end of a pair of worn tracks that wound through oak trees, oak brush, and scrub pine. It no doubt had once been someone's dream, but now it was just another minor nightmare of disintegrating shingles, sagging porch, and cluttered yard. A battered moped leaned against a wall, and there were a half-dozen pretty good automobiles scattered like cards in the clearing surrounding the house. As Professor John Skye and other university faculty have observed more than once, you can always tell college students from their teachers because the students have the new cars.

The house looked to have only two or three small bedrooms, but clearly was filled with unofficial sleepers who didn't mind violating Edgartown's zoning laws and health codes. As long as they didn't get too loud and annoy their neighbors, the cops would leave them alone, having other, more important matters to attend to. Ben Krane, who already had gotten his gigantic summer rental fee up front, didn't care either.

It was midmorning, but nobody seemed to be up. I

parked and went to look at the moped. It was definitely Adam Washington's. I climbed onto the creaking porch and knocked on the door.

Nothing.

I knocked again, louder.

I heard muffled groans and some foul language, then the squeak of footsteps coming to the door.

A bleary face blinked at me.

"I want to talk to Adam Washington," I said.

The face's mouth moved and a noise came out. It sounded sort of like that of a strangling cat. The face tried again. This time I thought I heard actual words.

"He's asleep. I'll tell him you're here."

She turned and went off somewhere, yawning rather noisely. The future of the world, which all too soon would be in her hands and those of her peers, seemed imperiled.

I peeked through the half-opened door into a dark, cluttered room with peeling walls and soiled carpet. I waited and heard more muffled sounds and voices, then footsteps coming unsteadily toward the door. The door opened wider and Adam Washington stood there, swaying and red-eyed, in a pair of jeans that hung from his hips like drying sails.

"Wha . . . ?" said Adam, trying to focus those bloodshot eyes.

"I want to talk with you," I said.

He got his eyes working and saw who I was. He stepped back but I got a foot in front of the door in case he was thinking of shutting it. I stepped close to him. "We can talk out here alone or in there with your friends," I said, feeling impatient. "I don't give a damn which."

His head was still half filled with sleep, and he hesitated.

"Shut up out there," mumbled a foggy voice. "Go party someplace else, for God's sake."

"I'll come out," said Adam, and did that, shutting the door behind him and blinking at the daylight. His face had a tired, worn look that aged him beyond his years.

"What do you want?" he asked in a sulky voice.

"You know Peg Sharp?"

"Yeah."

"You know Linda Carlyle and Perry Jonson?"

He got coy. "Maybe."

I tried a tough voice. "No maybe about it, Adam. You know both of them."

He wavered. "So what?"

"Where are they?"

He thought the noose was loosening and relaxed a bit. "Down south someplace. I haven't seen them for months."

"I need an address and phone number."

He shook his head. "I don't know either one."

"But you know where Millicent Dowling is. I want to talk with her, too."

He flared. "You keep her out of this!"

I pretended to flare back. "Fat chance, Adam. You're all in this together, one way or another."

"Millie doesn't have anything to do with anything."

"Where is she?"

He shook his head and gave me a complex look that I couldn't quite decipher. There was anger and fear in it, and maybe some guilt mixed with stubbornness and pride. I picked on the guilt and fear.

"There's an arson inspector on this case and insurance investigators are on their way if they aren't here already. There's a body lying in a lab over on the mainland, and there are some guys in homicide just waiting for the autopsy results. Anybody who knows anything about these fires is going to be grilled by tougher people than me, so if you know anything you'll be smart to start talking now, before you and your friends end up charged with murder and arson!"

It was a tough-sounding speech and it seemed to work, for to my surprise Adam Washington began to cry.

23

Washington's tears rolled from his swollen, red eyes, and he walked past me, out toward the Land Cruiser, sobbing. I went after him.

"I don't want them to know," he moaned in a little voice.

"Know what?"

"What happened."

"What did happen?"

His voice was watery and he was gulping for air. "It was my fault. I don't want them to know."

"What do you mean it was your fault?"

"You know, or you wouldn't be here!"

I thought hard but could only come up with one possibility. "You mean the moped. What about it?"

"You know already. I loaned it to her. If I hadn't, she couldn't have done it! If they find out, they'll blame me, just like you're doing!"

"I'm not blaming anybody for anything yet," I said in what I hoped was a comforting voice. "Now, take your time and tell me exactly what happened."

He wiped at his nose with his forearm and flashed worried eyes at the house. "They won't be like you. You didn't lose anything in the house; they lost everything they had, and they'll blame me."

There seemed to be plenty of guilt in his group. The boy I'd seen at the ruin had been full of it, too.

"Tell me what happened. Start with the girl. Who borrowed the moped?"

"Why, Millie, of course."

"Millicent Dowling?"

My brain was full of half-formed ideas.

"Yeah." He nodded. "Millie. She borrowed the moped just like before. But this time she didn't bring it back."

"I know. I saw it leaning against a tree there, where the last house burned down."

He nodded. "Yeah. I went down there later and found it and drove it back here." He wiped at his eyes. "I didn't want the cops or whoever to get it. I thought they'd trace it back to me and know I was involved, and then they'd find out Millie did it. I didn't want that, but now here you are anyway, so what good did it do me? Now everybody will know."

"But you didn't think she did it until afterward, did you?"

"No! But now—"

I interrupted. "You say Millie borrowed the moped another time. When was that?"

"When the other fire started." He suddenly gave me a cagey look. "Say, maybe I shouldn't be talking to you about this."

"You'll talk to somebody," I reminded him. "But maybe you're not in this as deep as you think. Maybe you're just an innocent guy who tried to do a friend a favor. Millicent Dowling is a friend, isn't she?"

He grasped at the straw. "Yeah. We're very close."

"Of course. So you were glad to loan her your moped as a favor."

"Yeah, I was. Both times I offered to drive her to wherever she wanted to go, because the bike's kind of tricky to start sometimes. But she said she'd rather go alone, so I said okay, started up the bike for her, and she went off."

"Where to?"

"To spend the night with her grandparents, just like last time."

"Her grandparents?"

"Yeah. They live in OB. She goes to see them now and then."

"What's their name?"

It was too early in the morning for a poser like that, but Adam tried to think. "Box, maybe?"

"Box?"

"Something like that," said Adam, wiping an arm across his nose. "I think that's it. Or maybe not . . ."

"So she borrowed it earlier this week, the night of the first fire?"

"Yeah. Then, when we heard about the fire, I got worried. But then she showed up the next morning."

"Did she talk about the fire?"

"She said she heard the sirens clear up in OB."

"Do you think now that she started the two fires?"

He began to fall to pieces again. "Jesus, I don't want to think that, but that's where I found the moped, so she must have been there. Somebody got killed in that fire!"

"Where's Millie now?"

He shook his head. "I don't know. She didn't come home, and I haven't heard from her. What I'm afraid of is . . . is . . ."

He couldn't say it, so I did. "That the body in the fire was hers?"

"Yeah. Yeah, that's what I think. Jesus, she's such a beautiful girl! I love her!" The sobs began again, as tears came down from his eyes like warm rain. I dug out my handkerchief and gave it to him. He held it against his face while his shoulders shook.

When I thought he was ready, I said, "We don't know yet who that body belongs to, but there's a good chance it wasn't Millie Dowling. Do you know where her grandparents live in OB?"

"I don't know. But Millie and Linda used to talk about how it was neat that the three of us were friends just like our grandparents were."

A little web began to form out of the individual strands of my thoughts. "Linda who?" I asked.

"Linda Carlyle. You just asked me about her. She was a

girl who worked here last year. We all sort of hung out together."

"You and Millie hung out with Linda Carlyle and Perry Jonson?"

He gave me a quizzical look. "Yeah. How'd you know about Perry?"

"I heard about him from some other people. I heard that Perry got beat up trying to fight a guy who'd hurt Linda, and that he and Linda are still together down in Atlanta. You just told me you love Millie. How close were the rest of you to one another?"

He wiped at his eyes with my handkerchief. "Well, Perry and me were pals, but Millie and Linda were like sisters, you know? They were like twins, even. I mean, not in the way they looked, but like they were on the same waves all the time. Millie was sick when Linda left last year."

"Are you all in college together?"

"We were a year ago, but Linda and Perry didn't come back this past fall. Linda was all messed up, and Perry stayed out to be with her. Or that's what Millie told me, anyway."

"Your grandfather's name was Ernie Washington. What was Linda's grandfather's name?"

He looked surprised. "Why, old Corrie's her granddad. Corrie Appleyard. I thought you knew that, being a friend of the family. Grandpa and Corrie have been friends since they were kids."

Free-flying bits of information began to hit the web forming in my brain. The bits were flies, and I was the spider. I could feel their vibrations as they hit, and wrapped them in webbing so I could devour them at my leisure.

"Do you know how I can get in touch with Corrie's family?" I asked.

"No. But I can probably find out from Grandpa."

I put a hand on Adam's shoulder. "Do that. And here's what else you can do. I want you to talk to Millie's friends. If she's staying with one of them, I want to talk with her. If she's not, I want you to find out her grandparents' name and where they live. She must have mentioned it to somebody."

He nodded. "Okay." He didn't seem very willing to defend his guess that their name was Box.

"The quicker, the better," I said. "I'm in the telephone book. Call me as soon as you find out something."

Another nod.

"And don't worry about being to blame for this mess. You're not, as far as I can see. You're just a friend who loaned his moped to a girl."

I got the number of the phone in the house, left Adam Washington to his thoughts, hopes, and fears, and drove home. There, I looked in the phone book for someone named Box. No luck, but no surprise, either. I tried directory assistance. No luck again.

Box? How had he come up with a name like that?

I walked out and looked at my construction project. It was as incomplete as my thoughts about the arson case, but while I was stymied by the case, I could at least make progress on the kids' rooms, so I got my tools and went to work.

Joshua, the helper child, wearing his small carpenter's apron, banged on some nails and held the far end of boards I sawed. He hit his hand with his little hammer, cried just like a lot of grown-up men would like to do under the same circumstances, and got needed sympathy and first aid from his mom, Nurse Zee, who eyed me with a sardonic and skeptical gaze when I told him that such injuries were all in a day's work for a builder and that with practice he'd stop hitting himself so often. To appease his mother, I also told him he could quit for the day if he wanted to, but he was soon back at his pounding and board holding. Such a manly little chap.

As I worked on a wall, keeping an eye on my assistant just in case he did try to do something really dangerous, like use my power saws, I was reminded of the Quick Erection Company and wondered how things were going with Susanna Quick and Mr. Black.

There seemed to be far too many predatory males on the island of late, and I was frustrated and irked by the thought of them. With luck, I might at least identify Susanna's stalker before too long, and with even more luck I might put him out of business. The Krane brothers, on the other hand, were probably beyond my scope, because they dealt with grown-up women, who, it could be argued, were consenting partners in their practices. I might think the Krane boys were feral and their women were victims, but they were all adults and responsible for their own actions, and that, according to my value system, made their relationships none of my business.

It wasn't the first time my thoughts and my emotions failed to agree, and it wasn't the first time the conflict gave me grief.

I worked until noon and made some progress with, or in spite of, Joshua's help, then took a break for lunch.

We ate out on the lawn tables under the yellow sun. On the far side of the distant barrier beach we could see the white sails moving over the dark blue waters of Nantucket Sound. It was a lovely island day, with the wind whispering through the trees. It said nothing of arson or other evils, but spoke only of beauty and gentleness.

Joshua, tired from his morning's work and full of food, decided to nap right there in his chair, and fell instantly asleep, the way innocent children often do, but corrupt adults rarely manage.

I picked him up and carried him inside to his bed, so the summer sun wouldn't burn his tender hide. Then I went back and cleared the table of plates and glasses and returned yet again to sit beside Zee, who was holding her daughter in her lap, but looked like she might have something to say to me.

She did.

24

Diana the Huntress, having had a busy morning of her own, nodded sleepily on Zee's lap.

"Before I met you," Zee began, "I dated other men."

I held up a hand. "I know that. You don't have to tell me anything about it. Your life before we met is your business, not mine. It has nothing to do with us."

She nodded. "I know we both agreed to that, and that's the way I want it to be, too. But sometimes—now, for instance—the past creeps into the present. I don't want it sneaking between us, so I need to tell you some things."

I opened my mouth, then shut it, then opened it long enough to say, "All right."

She bounced Diana gently on her knee, watching her daughter's eyelids grow heavy. I felt a sense of sanctity as I looked at the two of them. Madonna and child.

"When Paul divorced me," said Zee, "I was a total wreck. I felt worthless. I came down here and lived with my aunt Amelia while I tried to put myself back together. You know about that, and you know that she helped me a lot, and that after a while, I began dating. What you don't know is that I wasn't very stable, and I did some foolish things with men." She raised her great, dark eyes to mine. "Ben Krane and his brother were two of them. I must have been just the sort of fragile woman they look for. I was with Ben first, then he handed me on to Peter. They treated me like chattel, and that seems now to have been how I saw myself at that time: like a worthless thing that could be owned or thrown away by anybody."

A small red glow appeared deep in my psyche. I knew it of old; it was the beast that lives within us all, beneath the thin veneer of civilization. I feared it and used my will against it. But it wouldn't go away.

Zee ran a hand through her long, blue-black hair, pushing it back from her forehead as though to give more freedom to her voice and thoughts.

"Ben is very conventional about what he wants from women. Mostly, it's just dominance. Once he establishes that, and exercises it for a while, he gets bored with the woman and wants another one. Peter is very happy to take over.

"Peter has a conventional marriage in New York, but he comes to the Vineyard so he can have women do things his wife doesn't do. What he wants is very humiliating for the women, but some of them want that. Others find out they don't. I was that kind. I did what Peter wanted for a while, but then, somehow, I realized one day that I was being a fool, and I left."

Diana was a rag doll, snoozing in her mother's arms. I wondered if somewhere deep in her subconscious she was recording the words being spoken.

"I was embarrassed and ashamed and angry," said Zee. "I blamed Ben and Peter at first, but most of all I was angry at myself. That all happened a long time before I met you, and I thought I'd put it all behind me, but then you took this job."

I was caught between her voice and the crimson fury pulsating on the margins of my consciousness.

A crooked smile appeared on Zee's face. "And then I was angry with you for taking this job. And when you wouldn't give it up, I was angry with everything. It was terrible."

"You should have told me then." The words sounded to me as though they came from someone living in a cave.

"No. Because in the past two days I've finally realized that I had no business being mad at you or Ben or Peter or myself; I was angry about something that happened between other people long ago, people who aren't here now."

My barbed-wire voice said, "The Krane boys are still here."

She shook her head. "But the person I was then isn't around anymore. She was sick, but she got better and now she's long gone. What happened then has nothing to do with now. I'm not that girl anymore and I haven't been for a long time. I think Ben and Peter Krane were wretched men then, and that they probably still are, but they have nothing to do with me. I'm free of both of them and that girl, too." She looked at me. "And I want you to be free of her and them."

I said nothing.

"I mean it," she said. "I told you about this so you'd understand. I'm a different person, and my life is different now. And I'm living it with you. It's you I love, and I don't care if you work with Ben Krane or not. He means nothing at all to me." She rocked Diana in her arms. "The world is full of men like the Kranes, and it always will be. They're a dime a dozen, and not worth a heavy sweat or a second thought."

I sat and said nothing.

"I'll put the babe in her bed and be right back," said Zee.

While she was gone I thought of her courage in telling me what she had told, and doubted if I'd ever tell her of some of my own early activities. I set my will against the red glow and drove the beast away, or at least out of sight. If I couldn't rid the world of its evils, I could at least try to rid myself of some of those in me. When Zee got back, it was my turn to talk.

"All right," I said, "I won't think about what happened back then, but I have to think about what's happening now. Ben and Peter are still up to their old tricks, and those tricks may have a lot to do with these fires."

"If you find evidence that will nail Ben and Peter to the wall, it'll be just fine with me, because I think they're scum. I just don't want you to do it because of what happened to me."

"I won't," I said, hoping it wasn't a lie.

We looked at each other and I saw that she was smiling. She suddenly no longer seemed sacred and pure, but divinely profane and totally feminine; no longer Mary, but Eve. It was a cleansing, familiar, carnal feeling I often got when seeing her.

"I like being married to you," she said.

My pulse beat in my veins. "Ditto, Brother Smut."

"Where did that phrase come from, anyway?"

"I don't know. My dad used to say it."

"I love having a couple of little Jacksons."

"What this world needs is more Jacksons; no doubt about it."

"As to that, I think it has just the right number."

I licked my lips. "Shucks. I was just giving thought to being fruitful and multiplying."

She grinned. "As Chanticleer would point out, we're shaped the way we are for delyte, too. Will you settle for that?"

I stripped off my T-shirt in reply.

"Gosh," said Zee, unbuttoning her shirt. "Right here in the yard?"

I kicked off my sandals and slid out of my shorts.

"What about low-flying planes?"

"The pilots will be so distracted they'll all crash. Not one will live to tell the tale. Here, allow me to help you slip into nothing more comfortable."

She allowed me.

Afterward we lay on the grass and looked up at the sky.

"You seem to have worked up a sweat," said Zee, running her hand over my belly.

"And you have some grass stains in certain places."

"The shower is big enough for two."

"Did you notice that Oliver Underfoot and Velcro were interested in what they were seeing?"

"They're very smart cats. But how do you know what they were doing? You were supposed to be looking only at me." She stretched like a black panther, arching her back, and flexing her shoulders.

"I'm looking at you now," I said and pulled her to me.

Later, in the outdoor shower that we use nine months of the year, I washed her long black hair and scrubbed her back and knew that life was good. I was hanging my towel on the solar dryer when I heard the phone ringing. I got to it just in time.

"How many times do I have to tell you that you should get an answering machine?" said Quinn. "I can hear you puffing all the way up here in Boston. You're getting too old for these frantic dashes."

"Nonsense," I puffed. "I haven't lost a step."

"I've got some information about your friend Corrie Appleyard."

My ears went up. "Tell me."

The information was that Corrie had married long ago, but, being a rolling stone sort of musician, hadn't spent much time at the Mississippi home place where his wife still lived. He was there from time to time and sent money back when he had some. His visits had resulted in three children, two boys and a girl. One boy died in the Korea police action, the other was a musician in New Orleans, and the girl was a Philadelphia physician.

Hearing that, I interrupted. "Did she marry a guy named Carlyle?"

"You know about that? Yeah. They have a daughter. Kid's in college."

Not anymore. "What else do you have?"

He had a synopsis of Corrie's professional life, which included a good deal of time in Philadelphia a generation ago.

When he was through, I asked him for any family

addresses he might have. He didn't have any, but he had the names of Corrie's wife and children. I wrote them down and asked him to mail the rest of his information to me.

"Hell, I'll just fax it. Oh, no, I won't. You, naturally, don't have a fax machine. Get with it, J.W.! This is the twentieth century you're living in, for God's sake. Get yourself into the electronic age! Stop sending messages by smoke signals!"

"You can fax it, if that'll make you happy." I gave him the number of a place in Edgartown where fax people can practice their odd communication habits.

"Don't spend all of your time on this business," he said. "Get to work on that addition. Brady and I are serious about fishing in the derby this year, and we'll need that room your kids are using now!"

"I may have Brady down, but I'm not sure about you," I said.

He hung up and I dialed directory assistance. Hattie Appleyard lived on a farm just outside of Port Gibson, Mississippi. The operator gave me her number. I dialed again and got the number for Dr. Emily Carlyle in Philadelphia. I called the Edgartown police station and left both numbers and the names that went with them for the chief to pass on to the Dingses.

I'd let the professionals ask Corrie's daughter and his aging wife for the name of his dentist or for other information that might help them identify the body found in the burned house. I wasn't up to that sad task, however much I'd be interested in what they learned. I had a job that was closer at hand. I wasn't sure that it would work out, but it was worth a try.

Zee, wearing nothing but a towel wrapped around her hair, came into view. Venus without the shell. My rarely well-behaved hormones began to stir once again. Had someone slipped Viagra into my beer?

"What's up?" she asked. "Oh, I see."

"I was going to drive to Oak Bluffs," I said. "But maybe I'll wait until later." I took a step toward her.

Just then, however, Joshua came into the room, rubbing his eyes. He was used to seeing naked parents, but his appearance curtailed my plan. He had apparently overheard my reference to Oak Bluffs.

"Can I go with you, Pa?"

Zee laughed and went into the bedroom.

"Sure you can," I said to Josh. "Just let me get into some clothes." I followed Zee.

"What are your Oak Bluffs plans?" asked Zee, as we slid into shorts and shirts.

"I thought I'd go see Cousin Henry Bayles."

Her eyes widened. "I'm not sure that's the best idea you ever had," she said, frowning.

"I'm not sure, either," I said, "but I'm going. I don't think Cousin Henry will loose his dogs of war on me as long as I don't get sassy."

"Maybe you should leave Joshua at home."

"I think he'll be okay."

She started to say something logical, but settled for another frown. Mothers have a tough time in this world.

Five minutes later, Joshua and I were on our way.

25

The first time I ever saw Cousin Henry Bayles was about the same time I first met Corrie Appleyard, only I met Corrie in Somerville, and saw Cousin Henry on the Vineyard. I was a kid, and my father and I were walking down Circuit Avenue in Oak Bluffs. My father, who from time to time tried to teach me useful lessons about life, pointed out the little brown man to illustrate the dangers of starting fights with people you didn't know. Cousin Henry was a scrawny, aging guy who looked like the wind could blow him away, but according to my father he was probably the most dangerous man I'd ever meet, being the prime suspect in the violent deaths of a lot of very big, very tough guys during the Philadelphia black gang wars before he had abandoned his life as crime boss there and retired quietly to Oak Bluffs. Later, when I worked on the Boston PD, old-timers on the force had told similar harrowing tales about Cousin Henry, whom they included in the almost mythical tradition of Capone, Bonnie and Clyde, and other killers held in high esteem by Americans who never had to deal with them in real life.

I had briefly met Cousin Henry and his wife after my own retirement to the Vineyard years later, but only because he was kin to the very proper and successful and wealthy Crandels, whose family had been coming to Oak Bluffs for a hundred years, and for whom I worked as caretaker of their big East Chop house during the off season. Cousin Henry had not encouraged me to maintain a relationship with him, and I could understand that, since he was not only picky about his friends, but he had damaged a lot of people in his earlier life, and had grown old only by being very careful about possibly vengeful acquaintances and visitors.

Now, though, I wanted to see him again.

He and the ageless little woman who was his wife lived in a modest house down by Brush Pond, on the banks of the Lagoon. The house was innocent-looking but well situated for defense. Cousin Henry had water on three sides of his property, so you could only reach him over land by approaching the front of his house, or by boat from the Lagoon, where he had a small floating dock reaching out from his beach. There was a porch overlooking the dock where a motorboat was tied all year long, just in case Henry felt the need to go to sea. All things considered, it would be very hard for any visitor to see Cousin Henry before he saw the visitor.

I wanted him to see me so he wouldn't be unduly nervous, so I drove slowly into his front yard, parked, got out with Joshua, and stood there for a while. After I thought I saw a white curtain move in a window, I walked with Joshua up to the door and knocked.

After a bit, the door opened halfway and Henry's wife stood there, looking up at me. She wore what women used to call, and maybe still do call, a housedress. The dress was a print of small flowers on a gray background, and its white collar was buttoned to her stringy neck. A stringy-looking hand held the collar of a very large, unfriendly-looking dog.

"Yes?"

I told her who I was and that I wanted to see her husband.

She seemed to give that notion some thought, then shook her head. "He's not available."

"Tell him it's a family matter."

"He's still not available." She began to shut the door.

I shot my last wad. "Tell him it's about Millicent Dowling."

The door stopped shutting and her small, dark eyes flicked back up at mine. "Who?"

I thought I saw a glimmer of emotion in those ebony eyes. I calculated generations. "Millicent is a friend of Linda Carlyle. Linda's grandfather, Corrie Appleyard, is missing and I want to talk to Millicent about it."

"You've come to the wrong place," she said, and shut the door.

As she did, I said, "Your granddaughter may be in trouble." It was a guess, but I had confidence in it because of the pattern of relationships I'd heard about.

The closed door looked me in the face.

Joshua, feeling my tension, took my hand.

I waited. Nothing happened.

So much for that plan. I was leading Joshua back toward the car when a voice came from behind me.

"You're Jackson," it said.

I turned and faced Cousin Henry. He looked not greatly different from when I'd first seen him decades before.

"That's right. J. W. Jackson. This is my son, Joshua."

"Bring the boy here."

I did that, and when I got to Cousin Henry, I said, "This is Mr. Bayles, Joshua."

Joshua put out his hand, and Cousin Henry took it. "How do you do?" said Joshua.

"Fine, just fine," said Cousin Henry, "and how are you?"

"I'm fine, thank you," said Joshua.

Cousin Henry released Joshua's hand and put his own toward me. I took it.

"You helped out Julie Crandel a while back," he said.

"I look after Stanley and Betsy's place when they're gone."

He waved at the porch overlooking the Lagoon. "We'll

sit. My wife is bringing lemonade." We stepped up onto the porch and sat in rocking chairs set below a window opened to the wind off the water. "Maybe the boy would like to go down and look at the boat," said Cousin Henry.

Josh was a fool for boats. "Can I, Pa?"

"Sure. Just don't fall in the water."

Joshua went down the path that led to the dock.

"Now," said Cousin Henry, "what's this about Corrie and my granddaughter?"

"So she *is* your granddaughter. I thought so, but I wasn't sure." I told him how Adam Washington had gotten his boxes mixed up with his bales.

"A container confusion." Cousin Henry smiled. Then his smile went away. "What's your interest in Millicent and Corrie?"

I told him about my father and Corrie's friendship, and about the fires and my conversations with Peg Sharp, Adam Washington, and the Krane brothers, and about the job I'd taken with Ben Krane.

"They found a body in the last house that burned," I said. "That could make it a homicide case, not just arson."

Cousin Henry's wife appeared with a tray holding three glasses of iced lemonade, put the tray on a table between us, and disappeared.

"Do you know who died?" asked Cousin Henry.

"I don't know for sure, but I think it was Corrie. They found his satchel beside the body, and it had some new pennies in it. Corrie did some magic tricks with new pennies when he was at my place."

"What's this got to do with Millicent?"

"I'm not sure, but I'd like to talk with her before the police and the arson investigators and insurance people do."

"Why should any of you want to talk with her?" asked Cousin Henry, taking a sip of lemonade.

I tried my own glass. Delish. There's nothing like cold lemonade on a hot summer day. On the dock, Joshua was looking down at the motorboat tied alongside. It was a bigger and better-looking boat than my little Seagull-powered dinghy.

"Because she was missing the nights when the last two houses burned," I said, "and the moped she'd borrowed from Adam Washington was found at the site of the second fire."

"What is the significance of that?"

"She borrowed Adam Washington's moped and told him that she was going to visit you. The moped was hard to start. She'd had trouble with it before. She told Adam she was going to visit you, but it looks like she actually rode the moped to the two houses that burned, then, at the last house, she couldn't get it started when she wanted to leave. If I were a cop, I'd want to talk with her about what she was doing there."

"But you're not a cop."

"I'm a friend of Corrie's. I'd like to know what happened to him."

Cousin Henry pursed his lips and looked at the dock, where Joshua was now giving thought to trying to get down into the boat.

"Do you mind if he goes aboard?" I asked.

Cousin Henry shook his head. "No, I don't mind. Are you suggesting that Millicent had something to do with the death of the person found after that fire? If so, and if that is Corrie's body, you are quite wrong. She's known Corrie Appleyard all of her life. She'd never harm him." He drank some more lemonade. "On the other hand, Ben Krane deservedly has many enemies, and any one of them may have set fire to his houses. That person would not have shared Millicent's affection for Corrie. Besides," he added, "if it comes to that, my wife and I will testify that Millicent was here with us when both of those fires started."

Joshua was squatting on the dock, wondering if he dared a leap down into the boat. I wondered, too, and got mentally ready for a fast run in case he misjudged and landed in the water instead.

"You're right about Krane having enemies and deserving them," I said, "but Millicent hasn't been seen since the last fire, and it may not be too long before people with badges start looking for her. I'd like to talk with her first, so I came here."

"I don't believe you can get the search warrant you'd need to look for her."

"I don't plan to try, but somebody official might."

Cousin Henry and I both watched Joshua jump down onto the deck of the boat and sprawl there. He was on his feet almost immediately, and looked back at the house. I waved. He waved back and then climbed down into the cockpit.

"As you know," said Cousin Henry, "I belong to a close-knit family. We take care of our own and are unhappy when others interfere with our lives."

"I do know that. I feel the same way about my family. But I am set on finding out what happened to Corrie Appleyard, and I think your granddaughter may know something about that."

"You mentioned that you're working for Ben Krane. That would seem to put you and me on opposing sides in this matter."

"Ben Krane wants me to find out who's torching his houses. If I find out, I may tell him and I may not, because if I'm right about his role in this whole matter, he probably deserves what's happened to him. But I don't feel that way about Corrie Appleyard. If he was murdered or died in that last fire, I want to know all about what happened and who else was involved. If that puts us on opposing sides, so be it."

His face showed no expression at all. "I will tell you one last time that my granddaughter would never harm Corrie Appleyard."

"I believe you. But I also believe Millicent was there when that last house burned, and I'd like to talk with her."

"I'm afraid that's not possible, Mr. Jackson. I believe your boy is too small to climb back on the dock by himself. Perhaps you should give him a hand."

I emptied my glass, got up, and walked down to where Joshua was discovering that he was, indeed, too short to get back up on the dock. He reached up with his hands.

"Help, Pa."

I knelt and lifted him up beside me.

"Thanks, Pa."

"Nice boat, eh?"

He nodded, obviously impressed. We walked back to the house. Cousin Henry stood up as we got to the porch.

"If you happen to see your granddaughter, Mr. Bayles, tell her I came by to talk to her."

"If I do, I will."

"And tell her that the authorities may come looking for her. They probably won't be long in learning what people have already told me, and they'll want to talk with her."

"You wouldn't be thinking of passing your information on to them yourself, would you?"

"No. At least not the part about Millicent." I put out my hand. "Well, good-bye, Mr. Bayles."

"Good-bye, Mr. Jackson." Cousin Henry shook my big hand with his small, bony one, then put the hand down and took Joshua's. "Good-bye, young man."

"Good-bye," said Joshua. "You have a better motorboat than we do."

"I'm sure yours is fine."

"We have a sailboat, too."

"I've never learned to sail, I'm afraid."

"My pa could teach you."

Cousin Henry's mouth twitched as a smile whipped across it and was gone. "I'm sure he could."

The sound of a closing door came from the front of the house, and a pretty young woman came onto the porch. Her skin was a golden brown, and her hair was black and wavy.

"I'm Millicent Dowling," she said. "I've been listening to you through the window."

I glanced down at her grandfather. There was a wry expression on his face.

"You're just like me, Millicent," he said. "You never do a thing you're told."

"I know. But after hearing what you both said, I decided to ignore your advice and come out and join the conversation." She gave Cousin Henry a kiss. She was inches taller than he, and it landed on his forehead.

Then she looked at me. "I'll talk to you, Mr. Jackson. Where should we start?"

"At the beginning, if you know where that is."

"I know where it began for me."

"Then start there."

26

We sat around the table on the porch, and Joshua sipped lemonade while the rest of us talked.

"First," said Millicent Dowling, "I want you to know that Corrie Appleyard is the man they found in the house. He didn't die in the fire, he died before it started. I think it was a heart attack."

I remembered the look of illness I'd seen in his face and the pills he was taking.

"I thought it was probably him," I said. "I'm glad he didn't die because of the fire."

"So am I, I—"

"Start from the beginning," said her grandfather.

I thought it an interesting interruption.

"All right," said Millicent. She had clearly been thinking about what she was going to say, because she didn't hesitate. "For me, it started a year ago. The four of us, Adam and I and Perry and Linda, came here to work for the summer. We were in college together, and when we discovered that all of us but Perry had grandparents who had been friends years before, it seemed almost like fate had thrown us together." She glanced at Cousin Henry, and as she did, I could see a hint of his bone structure in her face, and had the sense that something of his character was in her, too.

She went on. "We came down and rented a house." Her eyes hardened. "Ben Krane owned it, and he wanted a lot of money, but we figured that the four of us could swing it and probably save some money, too. We got jobs and probably everything would have been fine except Linda and Perry had a fight." She looked at me. "You know about that."

"I was told it happened. I wasn't told why."

"It started out just being a spat about Perry thinking Linda was being too sensitive about being black in lily-white Edgartown, and Linda thinking that Perry wasn't being sensitive enough, but one thing led to another until there was an explosion and Linda wasn't speaking to Perry.

"And just then who should show up, tall, lean, handsome, rich, and white as Moby Dick, but Ben Krane? And who should go off with him, just to teach Perry a lesson, but my friend Linda?"

People do apparently irrational things all the time, but sometimes there's a reason for their doing them, so I asked, "If Linda was sensitive about being black in lily-white Edgartown, why did she go off with Ben Krane?"

Millicent's face looked both angry and embarrassed. "That's exactly why she did it. Because he was white! She was going to hurt Perry by dating a white guy! Especially a rich, sophisticated white guy who could show her the good time that Perry could never afford. I tried to talk her out of it, but she was too mad to listen, so off she went, and moved in with Ben Krane."

"And how did Perry take that?"

"He was angry and miserable, because he and Linda had gotten very, very close during the year before, at school. He loved her. I loved her too, and I was just as mad as Perry was."

"And Perry kept on loving her. Enough to get himself beaten up by Ben Krane."

She nodded. "Yeah. And enough to stay with her now, down in Atlanta, while she gets herself together."

"How long did she stay with the Kranes?"

"So you know about Peter, too. Well, she was only with them for a couple of weeks, but it was enough. Ben took her places she wouldn't normally go to, restaurants and bars and clubs, and places like that. She thought it was because he was proud of her, but later, when he was through with her, she realized it was only so he could show off his latest conquest, his latest toy. It did something to her, something bad. She'd been a fool."

"People make mistakes," I said, remembering what Zee had told me. "We all do foolish things."

"I don't think you understand." Millicent Dowling's jaw tightened. "Linda's ancestors, mine too, really were slaves, and she hated the thought of what they'd been forced to do. And now she was allowing herself to be a white man's toy. She hated herself so much that when Ben Krane handed her over to his brother, she felt she deserved it. She did everything Peter Krane told her to do. She became what she hated and feared most of all, and when Peter got tired of her and sent her away, she came back to the house because she didn't have anywhere else to go, but all she did was cry. She couldn't work and we couldn't make her feel better. It was maddening! This beautiful, bright woman reduced to ruin in less than three weeks!"

The story echoed what Zee had told me. But Zee, being older and maybe tougher, had been strong enough to overcome her wounds. Linda had not, probably in part because of her own idealism.

Nothing is more mortifying for young romantics than failing to live up to self-expectations. We can forgive others for falling short, but we can't forgive ourselves. I was once again glad I was no longer twenty.

"And that's when Perry got himself beaten up," I said.

"Yes. Perry tried to fight Krane, but only got himself hurt. Krane laughed at him." Her eyes flashed fire.

"And then Perry and Linda left the island."

"Yes."

"And they haven't been back."

"No."

"But you and Adam stayed."

"Yes, and —"

"Stop," said Cousin Henry in a voice that I would have obeyed, had it been directed at me. Millicent Dowling's voice ceased. Cousin Henry beckoned her and she leaned toward him. He put his mouth close to her ear and whispered something, then sat back again.

She looked at him and a small smile appeared on her lips. "Yes," she said. "You're right." Then she turned back to me and most of the smile was gone. "A nameless someone has entered my story."

"I'd prefer a name, but I can live without one." I looked at Cousin Henry, who wore an enigmatic expression as he looked at his granddaughter.

"No name. But the story is true in all other respects."

"I'll settle for that."

Millicent Dowling sat and set her tale in order. "Someone without a name was very angry about what happened to Linda and Perry, and wondered what could be done. The Lord says vengeance is His, but someone didn't want to settle for that. This spring, then, before students started coming to the island for the summer, someone made a quick trip and burned down a house belonging to Ben Krane."

I held up a hand. "How did someone know how to do that and get away with it?"

Millicent cocked her head to one side. "Obviously you're not an Internet person, Mr. Jackson. You can learn how to do all sorts of violent things on the Information Superhighway. Bombs, booby traps, you name it."

"Arson tricks, too?"

"They don't have to be complicated. Last spring, someone soaked a sheet in gasoline and put one end of it in the oven of the stove and the other on the floor. Then someone poured gasoline on the floor, turned on the oven, and left. By the time the oven heated enough to ignite the sheet, someone was on a boat for the mainland."

Smart someone.

"Of course," said Millicent, "that technique only works

if the house is empty and nobody's going to be around for an hour or two.

"Someone thought that one quick trip to the island might not have been noticed, but that if such trips were repeated it was only a matter of time before some sharp-eyed arson cop or insurance investigator began to notice that whenever someone came to the island, another one of Ben Krane's houses burned down. So someone came for the summer when a lot of college kids do, and earlier this week went to another of Krane's houses, one that was empty because all of its occupants were at a party some-where else. This time, someone took out fuses, then shorted some wires, then put pennies behind the fuses and replaced them. The place was on fire before someone got out of the yard."

"I've heard about that trick with pennies. Is that another Internet tidbit?"

"I, of course, know very little about such things, but I understand that someone might have gotten that infor-mation off a computer." The words came from her mouth, but they could have as easily come from Cousin Henry's. Like grandfather, like granddaughter. Millicent Dowling's looks were as deceiving as his.

"The penny trick was used again the night Corrie died," I said. "The Dingses, the arson investigators, told me that there were new pennies behind the fuses. Do you know anything about that?"

"You said Corrie played magic tricks with pennies at your house. He did the same at Adam's house, so we all knew he had those new pennies."

She paused, and for the first time it seemed difficult for her to speak. But then she reached into herself and found strength. "The night of the last fire, Corrie was supposed to have left the island, and everybody else in the house was at a party. Someone went to the house, sure that it was empty, but going from room to room, just in case someone was there. No one was, so someone went into the basement and removed the fuses and then shorted out wires as before." Another pause, another gathering of strength, then: "But as someone was at the fuse box, she . . . he heard footsteps on the stairs, and there was Corrie. He'd been waiting to catch the shuttle bus to the boat, but had gotten sick and come back to the house to lie down. When he heard someone in the basement, he'd come down and instantly seen what someone was up to.

"There had been enough burnings, he said, and if there were more, someone would surely be caught or hurt. He said enough damage had already been done, and there was no need for more."

Millicent's face was like stone. "Someone said there was no saving this house, but for Corrie's sake there would be no more. Corrie said in that case, he would fire the place himself, so someone would bear no blame. He got out his new pennies and started for the fuse box, but then he fell down and when someone went to him, he was dead. Someone tried to revive him, but it was no use. Then she . . . he tried to lift him, to carry him out of the house, but he was too heavy. Someone then thought of the Viking funerals and decided that it was as good a way for a hero to die as any other. So someone put Corrie's pennies in the fuse box, then took his guitar out of the house so something of him would be saved. When the fire was going well, someone went away."

She looked at me with deep eyes I couldn't read.

"You couldn't start the moped, so you walked. Somebody can probably testify to seeing you."

She shrugged. "Someone got a ride with a guy trying to catch the next boat off island. He's home in New York by now."

"What about all the stuff that belonged to the people living in those houses? They lost everything."

Another shrug. "Someone had seen their stuff. It was

college junk, mostly. Of no value compared to what happened to Linda."

I ran things through my mind, as Cousin Henry and his equally tough-minded granddaughter watched me with hooded eyes.

"Why did you decide to tell me this?" I asked.

"A good question," said Cousin Henry, giving Millicent Dowling a crooked smile.

She lifted her chin. "Some people will think Corrie did it. It's what he wanted them to think, but I wanted you to know what really happened."

"Why me?"

"Because Corrie told me I could trust you if I ever needed help. He said it there in the cellar just before he died." She made a small gesture with her hands. "He was afraid for me, I think, and wanted me to know that Grandpa and Grandma weren't the only people I could go to, if I needed to. He said you were a friend."

I thought of the songs Corrie had sung: the blues, full of sorrow mixed with hope; songs of good and bad times, of loneliness and friendship, of down-and-out men and women, of the refusal of the soul to perish in the face of suffering.

"I hope he was right about you," said Cousin Henry, "because if he wasn't, my granddaughter has said some very foolish things here at this table."

"He was right about me," I said.

Millicent nodded. "I'm glad."

"This is what I think you should say if anybody comes to talk with you," I said to her. "Tell them that you borrowed Adam's moped so you could come here to spend the night with your grandparents, but that you rode to the house first to get something that belonged to you—a coat, maybe, something like that; you decide, but keep it simple. Tell them that you couldn't start the moped again, so you hitched a ride here. Don't mention seeing Corrie, and insist that you were here when you heard the sirens.

If you tell that story and stick to it, the chances are good that Corrie will get the rap."

I stopped and studied her face. It was a pretty, intelligent, almost innocent-looking face, but there was hidden dangerousness behind it.

"I'm going to make a report to Ben Krane," I said, "and I plan to convince him that Corrie was his arsonist. But before I do that, I want you to tell me that you'll be doing no more torching of buildings here or anywhere else. Corrie was right. There's been enough of that."

Her lips formed a smile. "You want me to agree to abandon arson? I've never admitted that I've ever engaged in it."

I smiled a grim smile of my own. "All right. But I think you know someone pretty well, and she seems to have a talent for the work. She can probably earn a good living at it if she makes the right connections, because in any big city there are people who want buildings burned down. I want you to tell me that you'll persuade her to give up that game."

Still the wry smile. "And you'll believe me if I tell you that."

"Yes. I think someone is a bright person who can probably make a useful life for herself in some other profession."

She thought for a moment, then said, "All right, Mr. Jackson, I'll do as you suggest. I think I can assure you that someone will torch no more."

Torch no more. It sounded like a book title.

Joshua had finished his lemonade and was back at the dock. I called to him and he came trotting back to the porch.

"Are you done talking, Pa?"

"Yes." I took his hand and said good-bye to Cousin Henry and Millicent Dowling. "Live well," I said to her.

"I will."

"You can do me a favor," said Cousin Henry unexpectedly.

I was surprised. "If I can, I will."

"I've never seen the famous Mr. Krane. I'd like to accompany you when you meet with him."

I'd had stranger requests, but none that interested me more. "Sure," I said. "I'll give you a call before I go see him. We can go together."

"Fine," said Cousin Henry, putting an arm on his granddaughter's shoulders.

I could feel their eyes following us as Joshua and I walked to our truck. I had mixed feelings and thoughts about what I'd discovered and agreed to. They weren't made simpler by Zee's first words when Josh and I walked into our house.

"Susanna Quick just phoned. She's gotten another call from that man. He wants to meet her tonight!"

27

I phoned Susanna Quick. She picked up on the first ring. "He called again," she said, in a surprisingly cool voice. "He wants to meet me tonight."

"Where?"

"There's an empty house off of Lambert's Cove Road. The people who own it won't be down until July."

"How do you know that? Did he tell you that?"

"No. I used to do housecleaning for them when we first came to the island. Later, Warren did some remodeling for them. They never come down before the Fourth. It's a great big place up at the end of a long driveway. It's isolated. That's probably why the guy chose it."

Probably, but a curiosity, too. "How does Mr. Black know about the place?"

"I don't know, but he does."

Hmmmm. "Did he give you directions on how to get there?"

"No. He seemed to know that I knew where it was. I'm supposed to go there tonight at ten o'clock, alone." She paused, then went on. "And he wants me to wear my Oriona costume."

"What did you tell him?"

"Well, I figured I could change my mind if I wanted to, but I did like you suggested and told him I'd be there. One problem, though, is that I don't have an Oriona costume. It belonged to the company I worked for, and after I left I imagine another girl became Oriona."

It was a problem I hadn't anticipated. "Can you put something together that can pass?"

"Well, I can try," said Susanna, "but I don't know." She thought a moment. "Well, maybe I can get some green tights and rig a little skirt. I have to look sort of like Robin Hood."

"Give the playhouse a call. They put on *Peter Pan* last year, and maybe they still have the costumes."

"I will. And I'll go to the thrift shops if I need to. Maybe I can find a tunic or something. Gosh, I don't have much time . . ."

"You'll need somebody to watch the kids this afternoon and tonight. Do you have a baby-sitter?"

"I'm not sure I can get one on such short notice. I'll try."

"Call John Skye's house. His twins, Jill and Jen, both sit for us and as far as I know, they're both at home. Tell them I told you to call them, and that it's an emergency."

"All right. I wish I had more time."

"What are you going to tell Warren?"

"That's one good thing. Tonight's his poker night. He plays penny-ante with some guys once a month, so he'll be out until about midnight. Do you think we'll be done with this by then?"

I wondered. A lot of things can go wrong even when a plan is well designed, and this one was hardly a plan at all.

"There's a good chance that'll happen," I said. "If Mr. Black shows up on schedule, you should be back home before Warren gets there. But your admirer may not show up. He may be just running a bluff or doing a test to see what you'll do."

"Oh, I never thought of that."

Other possibilities that I suspected she hadn't thought of were that more than one person might be involved, that Mr. Black and his friends, if he had any, might be more than I could handle, that things could go wrong in ways I couldn't anticipate.

"Are you sure you want to go up there?" I asked. "Maybe we should use a ringer."

"What's a ringer?"

"In this case, it would be somebody dressed in an Oriona costume pretending to be you. A policewoman, maybe, or a small man who knows how to handle bigger people." I thought of Manny Fonseca, Zee's shooting instructor. He wasn't very big, but he had killed two men that I knew of.

But Susanna would have no part of a ringer. "No, J.W., I'm going to do this myself. I want to meet this man, whoever he is, and give him a piece of my mind!"

"It could be dangerous."

"I'm not afraid! Well, maybe a little. But with you there, I'll be fine!"

She was a gutsy woman. Warren was lucky to have her.

"All right," I said. "Tell me how to get to the house."

She did.

"Okay," I said. "You show up there at ten in the best Oriona outfit you can put together. You won't see me, and Mr. Black won't see me, but I'll be there. When he makes his play, I'll make mine."

Bold talk is cheap.

"Good," said Susanna.

I hedged one last time. "Don't be afraid to call the whole thing off. This guy will call you again if you don't show up. You can count on it."

"I'll be there. I want this over and done with!"

"I'll see you there at ten, then." I hung up and looked at the phone.

Zee had been listening. "I'll call and see if I can get the other twin to sit for us. Do you want me to go up there with you as backup? I can get somebody to work for me, if you do."

The idea of a backup had never crossed my mind, but now that it was mentioned, it seemed very sensible, especially since Mr. Black might have some associates of his own up at the house. But I didn't really like the notion of Zee being up there.

She read my husbandly mind, as wives can often do. "I know you'd rather I stayed out of harm's way, Jeff, but Susanna doesn't want anybody else to know about this business. If you bring somebody else in, there'll be one more person to tell the tale."

"It's just that there might be trouble, and if there is, I'd prefer you weren't in it."

"And I'd prefer you weren't in it, but that won't stop you." She leaned on the door frame, lean and lithe. "We can take a couple of flashlights and a couple of pistols, too, if you think we might need them. Susanna's my friend, and I don't like this happening to her."

She pleased me. I said, "I have the impression that I'd have to tie you to the bed to keep you from going with me."

"Mr. Black's the guy who seems to want to tie somebody up. I don't think you're the type."

It was something of a surprise to me that there was actually no one I'd rather have with me than Zee, in spite of the possibility of danger. "We'd better find us a baby-sitter, then," I said. "We want to get up there early, before Mr. Black does. He knows the territory, apparently, and we don't, so we'll need to scout the area and hunker down out of sight before he shows up." I felt the corner of my mouth turn up. "I love you."

"And I love you," she said, reaching for the phone.

"Whatcha doing, Pa?" asked Joshua, as I gathered sandwich makings on the kitchen table. His sister stood beside him, a teddy bear under her arm.

"Making supper for your mom and me."

"Are we going on a picnic, Pa?" Both Diana the Huntress and Joshua were fond of picnics. Of course Diana, especially, was fond of food at all times in all forms.

"No, Joshua," I said. "Just your mom and I are going to have the picnic. A twin is going to come and stay with you and your sister and fix your supper."

A twin was at least as good as a picnic. "Which one, Pa? Which one is coming?"

An unfair question, since I can't tell the twins apart.

"Your mom is making the arrangements," I said, avoiding another revelation of paternal ignorance.

"Can I help make the sandwiches?"

Why not? "You can spread the mayonnaise," I said.

So Josh and Diana climbed up and smeared bread slices, themselves, and the tabletop with mayonnaise. When they were through, I put ham and cheese, sprouts, pesto, and lettuce between the bread slices. Sandwiches deluxe.

I got our little collapsible cooler and put the sandwiches, some half-sour pickles, some chips, and a couple of bottles of Sam Adams inside it. Then I filled a thermos with ice cubes and water, and we were provisioned for the night.

Zee came back from the phone. "Jill is going up to sit for Susanna, and Jen is coming here in an hour. I got Marcia Simpson to take my shift at work. Joshua and Diana, your faces are a mess. Come on. We're going to wash off that mayo so you don't disgrace the family when Jen comes."

The three of them headed for the bathroom, and while I collected a five-cell flashlight for me and a smaller plastic model for Zee, and put some bug lotion in my pocket, I thought about the contents of the gun cabinet.

Manny Fonseca, who loved guns beyond all things but his family, when asked why he toted one on peaceful Martha's Vineyard, inevitably replied, "It's better to have one and not need it than need one and not have it." It was a view I rarely shared, but tonight struck me as an exception, so I got out my old police .38, loaded it up and put it in its holster, and put both in a canvas backpack with the flashlights.

Soon Zee and her shiny-faced kidlings reappeared and I told her what was in the backpack.

A frown appeared on her face. "Guns are dangerous."

"Yes. I doubt if I'll need it, but . . ." I shrugged.

Zee had two pistols: the Beretta .380, which she had started with but didn't use much anymore, and the customized .45, which she now used in shooting competitions. Being a talented shootist who didn't approve of guns, she occasionally teetered on the rim of paradox and indecision.

"I wish I knew who was going to be up there."

I was no help. "Me, too," I said.

"I can't really imagine needing one."

"You're probably right. Probably all we'll need is the flashlights. Once we ID this guy, he'll know it's all over for him, and he'll leave Susanna alone because he won't want his name known."

Zee nodded. "I wouldn't want mine known."

I said nothing.

"I'm going to take the three-eighty," said Zee, giving me an almost-but-not-quite-apologetic look.

"Fine. You know what Manny always says."

"Yes, I do."

Two hours later we were in West Tisbury, hiking up a narrow, sandy driveway. The Land Cruiser was parked a half mile back, just off Lambert's Cove Road, where Mr. Black was not apt to see it. The driveway wound through trees that almost touched overhead, toward the top of a hill that promised a nice view of Vineyard Sound. The promise was fulfilled when we came to the house and barn. They stood in a small meadow surrounded by forest that fell away on every side and gave an especially fine view of the Elizabeth Islands.

We stood in the trees for some time, looking for signs of life. There were none. We walked out across the meadow and I knocked at the door of the large white farmhouse. No one responded. We knocked on the back door. Nothing. We went to the barn. A door was open, and we went in. No one was there, but there were well-maintained machines in storage: a small tractor with plows, harrows, and a wagon that went with it; a riding mower; a handsomely maintained De Soto sedan supported by blocks, the object of some collector's eye.

"He told her to come to the front of the house," I said. "I don't know where he'll be waiting, but I want to be close to her, so we should probably be in the house."

"But it's locked."

I revealed my picks.

"Oh," said Zee. "But isn't it illegal to pick locks?"

"Yes, it is."

She raised a brow. "Oh, well."

We went in through the rear door of the house and locked it again behind us, and then went to the front of the house. We had a good view from the living room windows on either side of the front door.

"We can wait for him here," said Zee. "When he comes to meet her, we can just step out and confront him."

"We can if he comes from somewhere else, but I think he'll come from in here."

"Why would he do that?"

"Because there are beds in here and not out there. I think he'll be inside when she comes and that he'll want her inside, too."

Zee thought, then nodded. "Take off your backpack." I did, and she got out her flashlight and the Beretta and tucked them into her pockets. "He must have a key," she said.

"Yeah."

"Where'd he get it?"

"Maybe he's the guy who owns this place."

"Would he have her come here? Would he do this in his own place?"

I thought of the serial killers who used their own homes as cemeteries for their victims. "I wouldn't," I said, "but people do strange things."

She looked around. "We'd better find a place to hide out."

We went through the house. It was filled with antiques mixed with simple, functional furniture. Whoever owned it had good taste, I thought. Also money.

"I think the pantry is a good place," said Zee. "We can hunker down behind the counter out of sight until he gets in, then catch him before he can get out. I'm starving. Let's eat."

All armies, even very small ones like ours, travel on their bellies. So we went out behind the house and ate our food and drank our beer, so there'd be no food smells in the house to rouse Mr. Black's curiosity when he got there.

If he got there. Maybe he wouldn't. Maybe he'd be lying in ambush along the driveway to catch Oriona, and any friends she might have, unawares. I didn't mention such imaginings to Zee as we sat uncomfortably on the pantry floor and watched the darkness gather.

I was glad I didn't when, just after nine o'clock, a key turned in the back door of the house, and someone came in.

28

I heard Zee inhale and felt the touch of her hand on my arm. Footsteps moved from the back door, through the kitchen, and past the pantry, following a light we glimpsed beneath the pantry door, toward the living room in the front of the house. Zee started to get up, but I touched her shoulder and whispered in her ear.

"We'll wait and see if he gets any reinforcements."

We sat. No one else came in. We sat some more and listened while the person I presumed was Mr. Black moved confidently through the house. Apparently he knew his way around and just wanted to be sure everything was as it should be. Twice more we saw light under the pantry door as he and his flashlight went through the kitchen. Then footsteps and the light came toward the pantry, and we squidged back as close as we could against the wall on the far side of the counter. I found the switch on my five-cell in case he spotted us. The door opened and his light flashed in and around. But it was only a cursory look, and then the door was shut and the light and footsteps moved away.

I pressed a button on my wristwatch and the face lighted. Nine-thirty. I released the button and the watch went dark. I liked my watch. It had cost me nine dollars and was shockproof, water resistant, multipurposed, and affordable if I lost it. You should never pay more than nine dollars for a watch.

My rump was not too well padded and was getting sore. On the bright side, I was now pretty sure that Mr.

Black was alone. I got slowly to my feet and flexed a few joints. I sensed Zee flow up beside me. The pantry was darker than the inside of a black cat. I flicked my flashlight on and off and located both the door and Zee's ear. I bent and whispered again.

"He'll be listening when she comes up the driveway so he can hear if she stops along the way to maybe let somebody out. If he hears her do that, he'll be ready to scoot out the back door. She won't do that, of course, but will drive right up to the front of the house. He'll be inside, watching. When she opens the car door, he'll be able to see that she's alone. She'll stand there, waiting. Then he'll have to decide whether to go through with his plan or to skip out the back door.

"I want you back in the kitchen in case he decides to run. You put your light in his eyes and yell 'Police!' That should stop him. If it doesn't, delay him if you can do it without getting hurt. Don't use the gun unless he comes at you with one of his own or a knife. If he does that, shoot him. Otherwise, let him go."

"All right." Good old Zee. No arguments when the chips were down.

"I figure he'll open the front door and have her come in," I said. "When she gets inside and the door is shut again, I'll put my light in his face and tell him the jig is up and get between him and the door. When you hear my voice, turn on your light and come to the living room making a lot of noise so he'll think there are several of you. Between us, we should nail him cold."

"All right. Be careful."

It was very good advice, but guaranteed nothing. Many a person has been killed while being careful.

I leaned down and gave my wife a kiss. Then I led her to the door of the pantry and slowly opened it.

Faint sounds came from the living room, where Mr. Black was apparently taking his stand. Stars and a half-moon cast light through the windows. Zee moved like a shadow toward the back door and disappeared. I turned toward the living room and tried to walk like a cat. Mr. Black would be nervous and any odd sound might spook him. I didn't make any odd sound, although I could hear the beat of my own heart. I eased up to the door of the living room and peered around the frame.

The window-light faintly illuminated the room, but for a moment I couldn't see Mr. Black. Then, a deeper darkness in the lesser darkness of the room, I saw him beside a window, looking out, motionless as an ebony statue.

Why was he so dark? Why so black? Then I remembered the picture Susanna had showed me of Oriona in distress. The figure distressing her had been a man in a black mask and hood, wearing a black cloak over a black shirt and tights. Mr. Black was dressed for the role of the distresser, and as such was apparently planning to again abuse the hapless Oriona.

Life imitating art, such as it was. It has long been noted that many criminals are childish in spite of their grown-up bodies. Although they age physically and even intellectually, they somehow remain eternal adolescents in their emotions and morality. Their sexual fantasies are those of pubescent teenagers who are driven by forces that are mysterious, threatening, thrilling, and irresistible. I didn't think that there was any cure for it, in spite of the claims of some psychologists.

The figure in the window moved, and I heard the faint sound of an automobile engine climbing up the driveway. Then, looking through that same window, I saw headlights through the trees. Then a car came across the meadow and stopped in front of the house.

The driver's door opened and a woman got out and stood in the pale glow cast by the dome light. She was wearing an outfit that belonged to Peter Pan. She held the door open for several seconds, then closed it and stood in the star- and moonlight.

Mr. Black stood looking at her for a while, then suddenly moved to the door and opened it. He flashed his light into her eyes, and I saw that she was wearing a mask and was dressed in green. Oriona garb, more or less. She put up her hand to shield her eyes.

He spoke. "Come here." It was a rough but somehow artificial voice. She hesitated, then came up onto the porch. He backed away and she came into the room.

"Sit there." His flashlight flicked to a stout wooden chair he'd brought from somewhere. She walked in the circle of light to the chair. He crossed around her and shut the door. Then he pulled the blinds and the room was lit only by his flashlight.

"Put your hands behind you and your knees together."

She was very trusting of me. She put her hands behind her and her knees together, and sat there as if bound by invisible ropes. Mr. Black's light lingered on her, and I thought I could hear him take in deep breaths. Then he walked behind the chair and put his hands on her shoulders. She shuddered. I thought that was enough.

I aimed my flashlight at his eyes and flicked it on. "Keep your hands in sight and don't move!" I said in as authoritative a voice as I could muster. "And don't try to run. The house is surrounded."

He froze, like a deer in the headlights of a car, his eyes wide behind the black mask he wore, his mouth agape. Behind me footsteps came running and a dancing light came into the room.

Mr. Black made a small sound, and Susanna flew out of the chair and across to me.

"Turn on the house lights," I said to Zee, "and let's see who we have here."

The room blossomed with light. Mr. Black's eyes went from me to Zee to Susanna and then to the door.

"Don't even think of it," I said, pulling up my T-shirt and revealing the holster clipped to my belt. "Sit down in that chair, and keep your hands in sight."

"Oh my," said Mr. Black. He sat down.

"Take off that mask and hood and let us have a look at you," I said.

He bowed his head, then slowly put up his hands and removed the black mask and hood.

Like Lawrence looking at the golden snake drinking at his watering trough, we stared with fascination.

Susanna was the first to speak.

"Warren! What are you doing in that costume? What's going on here?"

Warren Quick spread his arms, his face wide-eyed and miserable. "I don't know what to say. I wasn't going to do anything. I just wanted . . . want—" He shot to his feet, tore off his black cloak and spun around in a circle. "Look, honey! I don't have any ropes or handcuffs or anything. I wasn't really going to tie you up or . . . I just wanted to . . . to see you, to see Oriona. I . . . ."

Susanna seemed more curious than upset. "You're the one who's been making all those phone calls! Why?"

Warren Quick's voice rushed out of his mouth. "I wanted to, you know, to have you . . . I mean, to have you dressed up like her, Oriona, like you did before I met you. I saw you by accident on the Internet, and I knew it was you. I recognized your eyes even though you were wearing that mask she wears. It was exciting! I knew it was all pretend, but I wanted to pretend, too!" He pressed the sides of his head with his hands, as words failed him.

"Why, Warren," said his wife in a voice full of pity and affection as she went to him, "if I'd known you wanted to play Oriona and Man in Black, you should have just told me. I'll be glad to do it." She put her arms around him.

"I know it's a sin," said Warren, "but I can't help it. I saw you in that costume and I had to have you."

"You're my husband," said Susanna, "and I'm your wife. It's not a sin for us to love each other any way we want."

"You don't think I'm crazy? I went to the library in Edgartown and tried to find out what was wrong with me, but I couldn't."

"You're not crazy," said Susanna. "We can try it out and see if we like it. If we do, that'll be fine; if we don't, we won't do it anymore."

"Oh, Susanna." He put his arms around her.

I looked at Zee and she looked at me. She beckoned me into the kitchen.

"Well, what do you think?"

"I was afraid for a minute he was going to burst into song."

"Not that," she said. "I mean, what do you think about him and her? Should we get out of here and leave them alone?"

"I think that's up to Susanna."

We went back into the living room. The Quicks were still wrapped in each other's arms.

"Excuse us," said Zee. "Susanna, we're thinking of going home. How does that notion strike you?"

Susanna didn't let go of Warren. "That'll be fine. Thanks for everything. I'll talk with you later."

Warren looked at us with his teary eyes and said something I couldn't understand. Maybe it was another thank-you.

Zee and I collected our backpack and cooler, and walked out into the night, leaving Oriona and the Man in Black alone.

The beams from our flashlights danced in front of us as we walked down the dark, sandy driveway.

"I saw him that day in the library," I said. "I thought maybe he'd found out about Mr. Black somehow and was trying to figure out what made him so weird. But he was really trying to find out about himself. Poor Warren. It must be tough for a good, straight-arrow churchgoer like him to wrestle with kinky thoughts."

"I'll bet you never tried to find out why you have immoral desires."

"Absolutely not. When I have lewd thoughts I just try to enjoy them. I have most of them about you."

"I guess there are no unnatural acts," said Zee, taking my hand, "but people still surprise me when they do certain things."

"Me, too."

Together we walked through the darkness.

Then I said, "Like what, for instance?"

29

The next morning I called Ben Krane's office and got—who else?—Judith Gomes.

"I want to talk with your boss," I said.

Judith's voice was cold. "When he comes in, I'll tell him you called."

"Tell him I'll be there at ten this morning."

"I'm not sure he'll be in by then."

"Tell him I think I know who burned down his houses. That should bring him." I hung up before she could. Judith and I just couldn't seem to warm to each other. So it goes, sometimes.

"Did you happen to find a check from Ben Krane in yesterday's mail?" I asked Zee.

"Is the pope Mongolian?"

"I think there'll be a Mongolian pope before I get a check from Ben."

Zee smiled. "That means you aren't really working for him, because he failed to fulfill his end of the contract, or something legal like that." She was glad to have me not working for Ben.

I, on the other hand, wanted Ben's money since I'd actually done the work he wanted, and I could use his dollars to help pay for the addition I planned on finishing before the start of the derby.

"I'll see if I can persuade him to come up with the dough," I said. "Who knows, maybe the check is in our mailbox this very morning, just waiting for me to pick it up."

"Har, har!" said Zee.

Diana the Huntress appeared. "Where are you going, Pa? Can I come, too?"

"Sure."

Joshua appeared. "Can I come too, Pa?"

"Not this time. You went with me yesterday. Today it's your sister's turn."

"We can both go, Pa."

"No. You stay with your mother."

Joshua tried the crying game on for size, but to no avail.

"If you want to cry, it's okay with me," I said, "but you have to do it for your mom because you still can't come with me this time. I'll be home later and you can cry for me then if you still want to."

I picked him up and gave him a kiss, then did the same with Zee, then took Diana out to the Land Cruiser and drove away.

Diana was not a great conversationalist unless hungry, so I had to do most of the talking, such as it was.

"First we're going up to Oak Bluffs to pick up Mr. Bayles."

"Okay, Pa."

That was it until we got to Cousin Henry's house. There, I introduced the two of them. She put out her teeny hand and let him shake it.

"How many kids you got?" he asked me.

"Just the two you've met."

"You take one of them with you everywhere you go?"

"Sometimes both. I like having them around."

"I don't know," said Henry. "When mine were little I was doing stuff I didn't want my kids close to."

"Yeah, but you lived in the big, mean city, and I live on Martha's Vineyard, where all is peace and love. I admit there are times I want the cubs to be home when I'm out, but not too often."

"Peace and love, eh?" Cousin Henry shook his gray head and climbed into the Land Cruiser, and the three of us headed for Edgartown.

On the way, I stopped at the post office, just in case a miracle had occurred and Ben Krane's check really was there. It wasn't. I drove on into the village.

"Don't get here too often," said Cousin Henry, looking at the clean streets, bright gardens, and neat white and gray buildings of the town. "Pretty place."

True. Edgartown is the loveliest of the Vineyard's villages.

I found a parking place on North Water Street, site of Edgartown's ritziest addresses, and we walked to Ben Krane's office.

"If you prefer," said Cousin Henry, "we can each speak to Mr. Krane alone. What I have to say to him won't take long, in any case."

"No," I said. "I want you to hear what I have to tell him, so if it's okay with you, we'll go in together."

"It's okay with me," said Henry.

Judith Gomes, looking severe, remained seated behind her desk when we appeared. I looked at my watch. Ten o'clock on the nose.

"Good morning," I said.

"Good morning," said Judith.

"Please tell Mr. Krane that we've arrived."

Her brow furrowed. "I believe Mr. Krane is expecting only you, Mr. Jackson, not a group of people."

"My colleague Mr. Bayles and I will be appearing together today. Mr. Krane will want to hear from both of us. My daughter, Diana, is only an observer. Diana, this is Ms. Gomes."

Diana walked over and put out her hand. Judith Gomes, unable to avoid being polite, hesitated, then took it, but recaptured her own hand as quickly as possible. She then went into Ben Krane's office and came back to her desk. "Mr. Krane will see you now."

Our group of three went in and Cousin Henry shut the door behind us.

Ben frowned, then put on a professional smile, which he directed at Cousin Henry, toward whom he put out his big hand. "I'm Ben Krane. I don't believe I know you."

Cousin Henry accepted the hand and let it go. "My name is Henry Bayles. Mr. Jackson and I share an interest in your current problems with fire."

"Indeed?" Ben sat down behind his desk and looked back and forth between us.

"To be brief," I said, "I think I know who torched your houses."

Ben was immediately interested. "Who?"

"We agreed on a price for such information," I said, "but so far the check hasn't showed up."

He sat back. "I'll have Judith take care of that today."

"Actually, I'd rather have cash."

It was apparently not an approved word in Ben's vocabulary. "Cash?"

"Half a week's salary now, the other half when I finish my report."

Ben tapped his fingers on his desk and his eyes grew even harder than they normally were. "I don't think so. You'll get your money, but not until after your report."

"Well, I can't say it's been nice talking to you," I said, "but I don't mind saying good-bye, so good-bye." I got up, took Diana's hand, and started for the door.

"If you know who started these fires, it's your obligation to tell the authorities," said Krane. "I'll get the information that way, if you won't talk to me."

"I haven't any idea who started the fires," I said. "I'll be glad to so testify in court."

"That'll be perjury. You just told me that you thought you knew. Mr. Bayles is a witness."

I looked at Cousin Henry. "Did I say any such thing, Mr. Bayles?"

"As a matter of fact," said Cousin Henry, "I heard you say you didn't know a thing."

I went on toward the door.

"Wait," said Ben.

I turned.

"Sit down, J.W." I did, and Krane scribbled out a check

and then touched a button on his desk. A moment later, Judith Gomes appeared in the door. Ben waved the check at her. "Take this and cash it and bring the money here."

She took the check and went out.

"I won't be held up," said Ben. "I want my money's worth of information from you. If I don't get it, you'll be in court for the rest of your life."

"You'll get it," I said.

Ben turned his angry eyes to Cousin Henry. "Maybe you'd like to tell me what you have in mind, Mr. Bayles."

"I'll wait until Mr. Jackson has his say," said Cousin Henry mildly.

So we sat. I played patty-cake with Diana, then gave her a horseback ride around Ben's office.

Before long, Judith Gomes came back and gave Ben an envelope. He looked inside. "All right," he said. "Let's have your report."

Judith Gomes went back to her desk, and I put out my hand. "Let's have the money first."

He tapped the envelope on his desk, then handed it over. I counted the money. It was, indeed, half of what we had agreed upon for the week's work. I put it in my pocket.

"Talk," said Ben, his falcon face hard with dissatisfaction.

I talked. "You know the arson inspectors are a couple named Dings. What I'm telling you now is that the Dingses are going to find out that the person whose body was found in that last torched house of yours was a guy named Cortland Appleyard. Last summer you and your brother took turns humiliating Appleyard's granddaughter, a girl named Linda Carlyle. The Dingses are going to find out that Cortland Appleyard came here a few days ago and that while he was on the island, two of your houses were torched, including the one Appleyard was staying in. Maybe Appleyard was here last March, too, when your other house burned, but if he was, I can't prove it, and I doubt if the Dingses can, either.

"The Dingses already know that the arsonist who fired

this last house used new pennies to bypass the fuses, and I can testify that Corrie Appleyard had a satchel and new pennies when he came here last week. The Dingses found a partial roll of new pennies in the satchel beside Appleyard's body. They'll add all that up and name Appleyard as the arsonist, because he had motive, opportunity, and the technical skill to do the jobs."

Ben stared at me. "How did this Appleyard guy happen to die in his own fire?"

"He didn't. He had a bad heart. It gave out on him before he could leave the house. He was probably dead before the fire started."

"How do you know that?"

"The Dingses will get a report from the medical examiner's office saying that's what happened. They may have it now, in fact."

Krane's eyes narrowed. "How did you get that information?"

I sat back and bounced Diana on my knee. "I think the reporters in Washington call it a 'knowledgeable source.' You've got what you contracted for. You know who the Dingses will name, and you know there won't be any more fires. At least, there won't be any more set by the person who set these. I'd like the rest of my money now."

Krane was no fool. He stared at me. "You know more than you're telling. You're hiding something. I want to know what it is."

"You're imagining things, Ben. Just because you're a liar and a deceiver yourself, you think other people are, too."

He stood up. He was a big man. "I won't have that from you."

I looked at him over Diana's head, and felt once more the flickering of psychic fire on the rim of my consciousness. It was frightening and pleasing at the same time. The beast within was awakening. I realized that I wasn't resisting it as I knew I should, and I knew why: it was because of what Zee had told me about her and the Krane brothers. My voice seemed lazy and hazy in my ears. "Are you trying to threaten me, Ben?"

He was not a man who had reason to lack confidence in himself. He was fit and, if rumor was correct, more than willing to use his training in the martial arts. He was also a very sharp lawyer. If he couldn't beat you one way, he certainly could another.

None of which meant a thing to me. I began to look around for a place to put Diana, so she wouldn't get hurt.

Krane smiled a happy smile when he noted this, and started around his desk.

"I never threaten to do anything I can't pull off," he said. "Right now I hope you actually do start trouble here so I can beat the shit out of you and claim self-defense. And after they carry you out of here, I'll keep you in court for the rest of your life. You'll wish you'd never been born."

I put Diana on the floor and gave her a little push toward the door. "You go out and talk with Ms. Gomes for a while, sweetie. And shut the door when you go out, please."

Diana looked at me with big eyes, then did as I asked. My own eyes went to Ben Krane. When the door closed behind me, I stood up. I felt airy and almost happy.

"Just a moment," said Cousin Henry, stepping between us. His voice was soft, but both Krane and I stopped in our tracks.

Krane looked down at the little man and opened his mouth to say something, but Cousin Henry spoke first.

"I presume, Mr. Krane, that you know nothing of the so-called black gang wars in Philadelphia back in the sixties and seventies. Am I right?"

Krane frowned. "What are you talking about?"

"History," said Cousin Henry, handing him a yellowed newspaper clipping. "Please read this."

Krane hesitated, then took the clipping and read it.

When he was through, he frowned. "A mobster got himself blown up. So what?"

"He was an acquaintance of mine," said Cousin Henry, taking back the clipping and putting it into his shirt pocket. "Some people believe that I had some involvement in his death."

Ben Krane became wary. "What's this got to do with you and me?"

"Just this," said Cousin Henry in a voice that was innocent as a coiled snake. "Linda Carlyle and my own granddaughter are good friends. I already feel a certain resentment about your treatment of Linda, and I will take it amiss if you continue to harass other people for whom I have affection or with whom I have pleasant relationships."

Krane's lip curled. "Like who, for instance?"

Cousin Henry nodded toward me. "Like Mr. Jackson and his family, for instance. Or like the Appleyard family, in case you should consider bringing a suit to recover damages from Corrie Appleyard's estate."

"Wait a minute," I said. "I don't need any help here."

"You may or may not be able to hold your own physically with Mr. Krane," said Uncle Henry, "but you're no match for him in a law court. Am I right, Mr. Krane?"

"Right as rain," said Krane, regaining his composure. "And the same goes for you, Bayles. If you threaten me, I'll tie you in so many legal knots that you'll die in court!"

"Which brings me to my point," said Uncle Henry, unflappable. "Let me show you this." His hand emerged from a trouser pocket. It was holding a tiny silver pistol that looked almost, but not quite, like a toy. He pointed it at Ben Krane. "Mr. Krane, I am an old man who has seen a good deal of life, some of it fairly raw, as you may discover if you choose to look further into the subject dealt with in that clipping you just read. Now, although I am in good health, I probably only have a certain number of years left to me, and I have no fear of death. I mention that because if you try to sue or otherwise bother me or my family or my friends in any way, I'll kill you."

Silence rang. Krane stared at him.

Cousin Henry went on. "Of course I may go to jail, and your heirs may win your lawsuit eventually. But you, Mr. Krane, will be dead. Do you understand me?" He cocked his head to one side and looked up at silent Ben.

"You can't bluff me," said Ben, at last.

"I never bluff," said Cousin Henry. "But, of course, any bluffer would say that. It might be simpler if I just shot you right now." He raised the pistol.

"No!" said Ben, stepping back and raising his hands as if they could fend off a bullet.

Cousin Henry nodded and put his pistol away. "Good afternoon, Mr. Krane. I never want to hear from you again, but Mr. Jackson will expect the rest of his money in tomorrow's mail. Will you come with me now, Mr. Jackson? I have to be getting home, but perhaps we can buy your daughter an ice cream cone before we leave town."

All the anger had gone out of me. I waved at the door. "After you, Mr. Bayles."

We went out, leaving a white-faced Ben Krane behind us. I felt ethereal, as though I'd inhaled something illegal. The world was different in some fundamental way: more dangerous, more good. I liked it.

30

"So Cousin Henry considers you a friend, eh? I guess you should be flattered." Zee sipped her vodka and a little smile played around her lips.

"I think it was just a convenient word," I said. "I don't think Henry and I will be doing much socializing."

It was now July, and we were sitting on our balcony in the evening, taking a parental break from our children, who were down on the lawn looking up at us in hopes that we would change our minds and let them come up too. But we wouldn't. It was grown-up time for Ma and Pa Jackson; no children allowed on the balcony until we finished at least one martini.

Out on the sound, sails were leaning through the wind and powerboats were leaving white wakes across the dark water as they headed in for port. Behind us the summer sun was easing toward the western horizon. The Cape Pogue lighthouse was a small white vertical line on the tip of Chappaquiddick, off to the east, and on the far horizon was the dim line of Cape Cod.

"Still, it was an interesting choice of terms," said Zee. "What do you make of it?"

"I think he was telling me that he approved of me leaving his granddaughter out of my story and of not actually accusing his friend Corrie of starting the fire. Cousin Henry gives tit for tat." I leered at her bosom. "Speaking of which . . ."

"Oh, no, you don't," interrupted Zee, sliding away. "No tat offers, please. At least not until later."

"Rats." I sipped my Luksasowa. Cold and good. Maybe God was a distiller. It seemed possible. Why else would She have created grain and potatoes?

"What do you think Ben Krane will do, if anything?" asked Zee. "Do you think he believes what Cousin Henry told him?"

"I think Ben is a smart guy, even if he isn't a nice guy. He sent me the rest of my money, didn't he?"

"Yes, he did." Zee looked at the new wing, now greatly advanced toward completion through Ben Krane's monetary contribution. "And so far he's made supportive noises about the Dingses' conclusion that Corrie was the arsonist. The grateful house owner applauding the results of the official investigation."

"Right. I suspect that Ben followed Cousin Henry's advice and looked further into what happened to those gangsters down in Philadelphia before Henry took up the quiet life here on the blessed isle."

"And just what did happen to them?" asked Zee. "Were they retired with extreme prejudice, as I believe they say in the CIA?"

"Precisely so. In an interesting but never pleasant variety of ways. Like I say, I believe that Ben Krane, being at least as smart as your average bear, probably checked that out before deciding how to deal with Cousin Henry."

"And having done it, has concluded that Cousin Henry wasn't kidding."

I nodded. "Which is what I would have concluded myself."

"Smart Ben," said Zee. "What a bastard."

"Indeed, on both counts."

"I'm glad you didn't fight him."

"Me, too."

"You might have lost."

"It wouldn't be the first time."

"But then again, you might have cleaned his clock."

I remembered the red rage I'd felt and my willingness

to loose the animal caged inside me. I repressed a shiver. "Maybe. I'm glad it didn't happen."

"Too bad he'll be staying in the slumlord business."

"It's an imperfect world."

We looked out across Sengekontacket Pond, where, on the far side, the last of the beach people were packing up their cars and heading for home. They were no doubt sunburned and sandy but happy, as tourists should be when vacationing on an island surrounded by golden sands and warm, dark blue water. I thought it was a sight that Corrie Appleyard would have enjoyed if he could have seen it. Good old Corrie. Another blues man gone down that long, long road.

"What do you hear from your pal Susanna?" I asked. "How are Oriona and the Man in Black doing?"

"I swear," said Zee, shaking her head. "There's just no understanding people and the things that make them happy. Susanna says they're better than ever. She gave her Peter Pan costume back to the theater company and made herself a real Oriona outfit, and every now and then when the kids are asleep, she and Warren dress up and play superheroine-in-distress games. She says Warren gets quite passionate and she does too. Love can be weird."

"And they still go to church, just like before?"

"Absolutely. I guess the spirit and the flesh have become one."

"Good. I think that's part of the great master plan."

Then I thought of the Krane brothers and their relationships with women. The acts the Kranes performed were those of users and abusers, and offended me, whereas the same or similar acts between lovers such as the Quicks did not.

The Kranes and their ilk were apparently also part of the great master plan. If there was a God, His or Her or Its notions were sometimes too much for me to grasp.

Enough of such thoughts. I put them out of my mind and let the loveliness all around me fill my consciousness.

The universe might have no meaning, but it was awesome and grand and beautiful, and that was enough.

I finished my drink and set the glass on the balcony railing. Sharp-eyed Diana immediately saw it and pointed.

"See, Josh!"

Joshua jumped to his feet.

"Pa, are you done with drinking? I see your glass! Can we come up now?"

Caught. "In a minute. Your ma hasn't finished yet."

"I'm done," said Zee, and emptied the last drops into her mouth. "I've had enough of this peace and quiet."

"Okay," I said to the tots. "Come on up."

Our offspring galloped toward the stairs.

Zee put her hand on mine. "We have a good life, don't we?"

Small steps clattered up toward us. "Yes," I said. "Yes, we do."

"Even though it's an imperfect world."

"Even though."

I kissed my wife, and turned to meet our scrambling cubs.

RECIPES

"Be wary of any recipe over four inches long."
—J. W. JACKSON

STUFFED QUAHOGS

There are as many recipes for stuffed quahogs (hard-shell clams) as there are quahog stuffers. J.W. likes this one best. He rakes his own quahogs (mostly from Sengekontacket Pond), but you can buy yours at the fish market if you don't live on Martha's Vineyard.

24 large quahogs
1/4 cup ground kielbasa or linguisa
1/4 cup minced onion
1/4 cup chopped celery
1/4 cup chopped green pepper
2 cups fresh bread crumbs
Dash hot pepper sauce (optional)
Cooking spray
Bacon
1 sprig of parsley

Steam quahogs just until they open. Reserve liquid. Coarsely chop quahog meat in food processor or meat grinder. Mix all ingredients together, except bacon and parsley, moistened with some of the reserved liquid if necessary. Spray twelve cleaned half shells with cooking spray. Mound filling in each shell and top with a square of uncooked bacon. Bake on a cookie sheet in 450-degree oven until the bacon is crisp and the stuffing is heated through. Garnish with a sprig of parsley.

Serves four as an appetizer.

CREAM OF REFRIGERATOR SOUP

This soup is a kind of green vichyssoise, which comes out a little different each time you make it, depending on what veggies you have leftover in your refrigerator. It can be eaten hot or cold, but is always delish. J.W. prefers it cold.

> *3 leeks (white part, mostly), washed and thinly sliced*
> *2 medium potatoes, peeled and diced or thinly sliced*
> *1 large onion, thinly sliced*
> *2 oz. spinach, washed and shredded, and/or any other*
>   *leftover vegetables in your refrigerator (except maybe*
>   *beets, although they might be good, too)*
> *2 tbsp. unsalted butter or margarine*
> *3 cups chicken broth*
> *1 cup milk, scalded*
> *1/2 tsp. salt*
> *Dash white pepper*
> *1/2 cup heavy cream (you can use skim milk, if you prefer)*
> *Chopped chives*

Sauté leeks, potatoes, onion, and spinach in butter in a large saucepan for twenty minutes, stirring occasionally, until soft but not brown. Add any other leftover vegetables. Stir in chicken broth and milk; bring mixture just to the boiling point and remove from heat. Season with salt to taste. Puree through food mill or in food processor. Chill several hours. Stir cream into chilled soup and serve in chilled cups with a sprinkling of chopped chives. Serves four.

Scandinavian Fish Bake

This excellent dish is amazingly simple and tastes wonderful. J.W. is very fond of it for both reasons.

10 small onions
4 tbsp. butter
1 lb. cod or other white fish fillets (J.W. has also made it with bluefish and thinks it is just fine)
Salt
2 1/2 tbsp. flour
3/4 cup milk
1/2 cup water
2 chicken bouillon cubes
White pepper
1/2 cup light cream
1/4 cup grated Parmesan cheese
Dill for garnish

Peel and slice onions. Place in small skillet. Add two tsp. water and simmer, covered, until onions are soft and transparent. Remove cover and add two tbsp. butter. Cook until water evaporates. Place onions on bottom of oven-proof dish and cover with fish fillets (preferably skinless). Salt lightly and set aside.

Melt remaining two tbsp. butter and add flour, stirring until smooth. Add remaining ingredients (except cheese) and stir constantly until thickened. Pour sauce over fish and cover with grated cheese. Bake at 350 degrees for twenty-five to thirty minutes. Garnish with chopped dill and serve with rice or boiled potatoes.

Serves four to six.

ABOUT THE AUTHOR

Philip R. Craig grew up on a small cattle ranch southeast of Durango, Colorado. He earned his M.F.A. at the University of Iowa Writers' Workshop. He and his wife live on Martha's Vineyard.